False Start

McKay-Tucker Men Book 1

Marianne Rice

False Start
by
Marianne Rice

ISBN: 978-1511930499

Editor: Victoria Miller

Dedication

For Jen, the best friend a girl could ask for.
You're a beautiful, strong, devoted mother, sister,
aunt, daughter, wife, teacher, and friend.
I admire you more than you know. Thank you
for being my constant sounding board.
The world is a better place because of you.

Chapter One

"We need to talk."

Startled by the deep growl, Meg Fulton looked up to the towering stack of testosterone filling her office doorway and cursed the butterflies that fluttered in her stomach.

She straightened her posture, ran her hand through her thick hair in an attempt to put all the strays back in place, and then reached for the lapels of the suit coat that wasn't there. She felt vulnerable in her silk tank top and wished she had an extra layer to shield her from the menacing daggers targeted at her. Putting on the jacket would only make a spectacle of herself. The thin tank would have to do.

"Sure. Have a seat." She crossed her legs and attempted to smile. Inwardly, Meg groaned. *Connor McKay*. She'd noticed him on the football field coaching his athletes and had not looked forward to the expected confrontation.

He remained in the doorway, making no move toward the empty seats across from her desk. His blond hair was short, barely longer than the scruff on his face, and as she looked up she saw his eyes—a fierce, fiery blue filled with accusation and something that ranged between confusion and lust.

Meg stood and retrieved her suit coat off the rack,

slid her arms through the expensive fabric, feeling the need to protect herself after all. In three-inch heels, she stood at almost five-eleven, but he still had half a foot on her. "What can I do for you?"

"This *plan*? Not gonna happen." He didn't elaborate, just made his statement sound like fact.

Pompous, arrogant jerk. He was probably used to flaunting his muscles to get his way. The Texas A&M shirt stretched over his massive chest, making him appear menacing and…hot. Horrified she even noticed, she tipped her head back and raised her eyebrow. "Why do you believe it's *not* going to happen?"

His wide stance continued to rigidly occupy the doorway. "Season's already started. My players won't be benched because of a policy that might start half way through their season."

The stereotypical football coach was obviously not used to having a woman as a boss, but Meg wouldn't let him intimidate her. The job as principal at Newhall High School would be a challenge, but one she was ready to face.

"*Is*, not might. And all I'm asking—" She cleared her throat, "*telling* you, is to have your players who are in danger of failing a class spend a little extra time *working* on their academics. It's quite simple. If an athlete is failing a class, he or she must stay after school in the Intervention program."

"And spend less time on the field?" His lips drew into a tight line. "Not gonna happen. They need to be at practice or they don't get to play."

"School doesn't start for two more days, Mr. McKay. No one is currently failing. Inform your players to maintain passing grades and their role on your team does not change." Damn but he infuriated her. Between the baby blue eyes and blond whiskers on his face, he looked like he belonged on one of those giant posters

Abercrombie displayed at the mall than teaching in a rural New Hampshire high school.

"We already have a program in place, *Ms. Fulton.* Students have to maintain decent grades to stay eligible. You're making it damn near impossible for a kid to play. Cut them a break."

"Decent isn't working. Allowing students to fail algebra as long as they pass gym isn't doing them any favors. This program doesn't average grades; instead it requires students to pass all their courses. Students have been given far too many breaks and look where it's gotten them. Newhall High is close to losing its accreditation. The first step is quite simple. We just—"

"You think it's that easy?" He shook his head and rubbed his hand across his unshaven face, unintentionally—or intentionally—flexing his biceps with the simple gesture.

"That's why we're all here: teachers, mentors, peer support groups. That's our number one job—to teach. Number two, and always number two, is coaching. You must agree or you wouldn't be a teacher." Meg inwardly cringed. Making herself sound like a walking ad for higher education wouldn't earn her any points. She didn't mean to sound so stuck up, but Connor infuriated her. Or maybe it was her unwanted attraction to him that ticked her off.

His bright eyes darkened and narrowed. She thought the conversation had finished, but he stepped into her office, testosterone invading her personal space.

"And what do I tell my kids who have nothing going for them, no home life, no hopes of earning decent pay or a respectable job because they don't have a lot of brain power, but can make a difference on the football field? It's what keeps them in school and off the streets. In our neck of the woods, kids don't come to school dressed in designer duds looking for a decent education. They come because their home life is shitty. They come to play ball. And if they can't play ball, they drop out."

She didn't like the strength of his body or the powerful way he spoke. For sixteen years she worked diligently to stand tall in every room she entered, every situation she encountered, and she was not about to lose all she had physically and mentally worked for because of *another* football player.

"And what happens to these kids of yours once high school is over and they realize there's a real world out there that they're not prepared for?"

"Football, hell, all sports, teaches kids endurance, commitment, responsibility, and teamwork. Those, *Ms. Fulton*, are skills we all need in the real world."

She crossed her arms and smiled. "You're absolutely right, *coach*. And these kids will realize how important commitment and teamwork are by the example you set for them. By how well you work with others in the mentoring program and how *responsible* you are as a teacher and mentor by making each of your players responsible for his education."

"This program of yours may seem great on paper but I'm talking about real kids. Kids you don't know squat about. I know their families, their home life, their—"

She needed to get the man out of her office before she said something she'd regret. Lifting a thick three-ring binder off her desk, she shoved it at his solid chest. "Here's my data. I started this program at my previous school and helped four other districts begin similar programs. Feel free to read over my notes. We can discuss this further tomorrow." She turned her back on him and put her laptop in her briefcase.

She didn't need to look over her shoulder to ensure he left. The air thinned and cooled the moment he walked out. She had to smile when she heard him curse and slam the door to the main office. Round one belonged to her.

There were only three stoplights in the small town of Newhall, and damn if Connor didn't manage to catch them all. He didn't feel sorry for taking his frustration out on his players at practice this afternoon. It was a taste of what was to come.

After leaving Meg Fulton's office, he had headed out to the comfort of the football field, sun and sweat, and had been bombarded by all sorts of questions from the kids and his coaches. But damn-it-to-hell if he had any answers.

"Coach, there's no way I can pass chemistry this fall. You're not gonna bench me, are ya?" His star running back whined.

He had to remain semiprofessional so he sidetracked the team with heavier warm-ups.

"You're not gonna be playing at all if you keep flapping your gums more than those legs. End zone to end zone. Five times. Hustle!" The team groaned and pleaded for answers to their questions. Answers Connor didn't have. It had been easier to keep them busy and too winded for idle conversation. "*Go!*"

If this was any indication of what kind of year he was going to have, he might as well tell the team to hang up their shoulder pads and call it quits. Principal Fulton was tough and confident. Too confident.

Part of him hated her for it. Another part of him respected her. And another part…*damn.* He shouldn't be thinking about his new boss this way, but it wasn't his fault she had legs that were meant to wrap around a lover.

It wasn't often that someone needed to put him in his place. At least not lately. Though he was well known in these parts, he didn't take advantage of his stature unless it was to give back to his community. Connor considered himself a good teacher and knew he was an excellent coach. He didn't need stats, trophies, or awards to tell him that.

He cursed as an image of Meg lying naked in his bed, dark hair splayed around her like angel wings, filled his brain.

He steered his GMC truck into his garage and shut off the engine. Next to him sat the black binder she'd given him. All he wanted was to have a beer, sit on his couch, and catch the end of the Red Sox game.

He could hear Rocky barking as he stepped out of his truck. The second he opened the door, Rocky bounded out to do his business. Connor went inside, stripped on his way to the bathroom, and then took a desperately needed shower.

Images of long, lean limbs and dark, wide eyes flooded his mind and warmed his body. Cursing, he turned the shower nozzle and rinsed off with icy cold water.

Freshly showered, Connor grabbed a beer from the fridge and then reclined in his chair, Rocky at his feet. He took a pull on his bottle of suds. The cold ale tasted good going down. Sure, he wasn't catching the pigskin or dodging the lineman in the NFL anymore, but coaching high school kids was rewarding in its own right.

The black binder stared up at him from the coffee table. "Ah, shit." He reached for it and thumbed through the meticulously organized sections. Just like her office, her hair, her clothes, everything about Meg was in perfect order. Which made him want to rumple her a bit. The thought of her disheveled did weird things to his insides.

Sitting in his recliner gave him a direct view of the wall of windows and French doors that led out to an enormous deck overlooking Moose Lake. There were no fussy decorations in his house. While it had a man's touch, it didn't look like a bachelor pad.

The windows needed no coverings, the nearest neighbors were across the water and only visible with a pair of binoculars. He wasn't a slob. Every item in his house had a designated spot. Clothes, books, weights, food.

The black binder mirrored his kind of meticulous organization. *Shit*. The last thing he wanted to admit was that he had anything in common with his new commander and chief. He was neat. She had OCD.

Thumbing through the binder, he noted the dates—ten years of data. She didn't look old enough to be a principal. Hell, she didn't fit the principal mode, period. They were old, balding, and grumpy. Not tall, with large, brown sexy-ass bedroom eyes, and a sassy attitude.

The last section held her handwritten notes. They weren't dated, but they looked like notes for a class, her senior thesis maybe? Information he was sure she did not want him to see.

A yellow piece of paper fell from the binder and landed on the floor. Connor bent over to pick it up.

"Well, holy hell, sugar. What do we have here?

Chapter Two

The mirror in the small teacher's bathroom didn't lie; she was no Snow White. The bags under her eyes after the second day of teacher workshops, not even the official start of school, told Meg she was surely doomed.

Only one person could be blamed for her flawed appearance. She regretted letting her emotions get the best of her and thrusting her binder of research at the hulking Connor McKay. Her life's work. Why didn't she tell him she'd fill him in at their scheduled meeting?

Because the man twisted her insides and confused her usually focused mind. Meg Fulton didn't ogle men. Especially tall, muscled men. They so weren't her type. Not that she had a type.

After Connor left she realized her fatal mistake of giving him The Binder. The one with her notes, her research, her career. Original documents that couldn't be replaced. If the arrogant bastard messed with The Binder, there would be hell to pay. But McKay didn't seem the type to read through five inches of data. He probably spent his nights drinking beer in a sleazy bar and picking up bimbos.

Smoothing her pink, sleeveless blouse and giving her bun a reassuring pat, she picked up her briefcase, opened the bathroom door, and walked with distinct poise to the conference room. Waiting inside the cramped, sterile room and gathered around the long rectangle table sat the fall coaches. Eight men and two women. Even after all these years, she still had trouble being in the same room with athletes. Cursing her insecurities, she concentrated on her yoga breathing and willed her hands to stop shaking.

"Good morning everyone. I believe I have your names straight, but please correct me if I'm wrong." She sat in the vacant chair at the head of the table, smiled, and made eye contact with nine of the ten people around her.

"I have an outlined report of three other schools who implemented the same plan and the data that shows the significant change in grades and attitude among student athletes." She passed around the reports and waited patiently while nine coaches thumbed through the document.

Mr. Testosterone leaned back in his chair and kept one hand wrapped around his Texas A&M coffee mug and the other tucked under his armpit. He remained too calm reclining in the hard-backed seats and too sure of himself this morning. His eyes held a small gleam. Something was up, but Meg would not let him get under her skin.

"Ms. Fulton, can you tell me about this school's socio-economic status?" Claire Marsh, the field hockey coach, referred to page three in the handout.

"Sure. Example A comes from South Port High. The community is similar to yours except they are a coastal community. Many families rely on the fishing industry while your community relies heavily on farming and small businesses." Now in her comfort zone, speaking about numbers and data, she felt more relaxed.

For the next thirty minutes the coaches fired off questions, and Meg confidently responded to each one, reassuring the staff with specific examples and data. Pointing out improving SAT scores, lower behavior problems and improved morale among schools who instituted higher academic expectations on its athletes. Not one peep came from Connor. He sat at the opposite end of the room, waiting to pull the rug out from under her. She could feel it. Right when the meeting wrapped up and everyone started packing up, he spoke.

"I have one question for you, *Ms. Fulton,"* he said, drawling her name.

Lifting her chin to him, she said, "Yes?"

"Has it always been your…mission…to save athletes from academic failure?"

"No, not always." *Crap.* How the heck he had time to go through over three hundred pages of data in one night was beyond her.

"Hmm, interesting."

All of a sudden the room became exceptionally quiet. She knew what he was doing. He wanted her to know he found her old notes and papers and anxiously waited for her to jump to her own defenses. She wouldn't stoop to his level or play into his game.

"If that's all, you're probably looking forward to some time in your classrooms." Meg stood and dismissed the coaches. They all filtered out of the room, but Connor's relaxed pose didn't budge. His tanned, muscular legs were casually crossed and he balanced an empty coffee mug on his right thigh. "Mr. McKay, is there something you need to ask? If not, I have a dozen loose ends to clear up before the end of the day." She didn't wait for a response but brushed past him.

"Would one of them be continuing your vendetta against athletes? Trying to sabotage our entire athletic program?"

She stopped in her tracks and closed her eyes. *Crap.* She took a deep breath to compose herself and turned to face the enemy. "I am not trying to sabotage the program. I want our students to leave NHS with a strong academic background."

Slowly, rising from the chair, he handed her The Binder. "*Athletes give a bad name to schools. Athletic programs should be disbanded from all schools. Hippocratic Oath and Athletes. Random Drug Testing in Public Schools.*" He glared at her, his golden eyebrows raised in question. "Which thesis paper got you into grad school?"

"Those are old papers and are not relevant to what is going on here." She yanked The Binder from his grip.

"So. You hold no animosity toward student athletes or coaches?"

"No."

"Hmm. Good to know. I could use some advice, though."

"Really?" she replied sarcastically.

"Yeah. Tell me, what I should say to Nick Mathers? Our star quarterback has a learning disability and can't pass math for the life of him. What do I tell his single mom who is on welfare and raising four kids, praying to God that Nick earns a football scholarship so he can go to college? What do I tell her when I have to bench him because he can't ever make a practice because he needs constant tutoring in math to, hopefully, maintain a C average?"

The presence of teachers on the other side of the door and craning necks reminded her to stay professional. "You tell her you are thrilled that this year he will meet the math standards because he has a mentor and an after school program lined up for him."

"And football?"

"Let me ask you something, *Coach.*"

He crossed his thick arms and scowled.

"What do you tell Ms. Mathers when Nick gets injured his freshman year in college, can't play football, and is no longer receiving scholarship money? What do you tell her when Nick has to drop out of college because he doesn't have the academic drive he needs to succeed because his high school said barely passing with a D was enough? Football won't last forever, but his education will. You should know that."

"Touché, Ms. Fulton." His shoulders seemed to slouch, if that was possible.

"Is this the way you treat all your superiors? Don't forget, *Coach*, I am the principal here. If you have a problem with my policies or me, feel free to bring it up at the next school board meeting. If you plan on being a part of my staff, you better learn how to play by the rules."

The door didn't actually slam behind her when she left; thankfully, the slow release hinges wouldn't allow it. Storming off in a temper tantrum wasn't exactly the way she imagined her first few days as principal in the small town. She held her own until she got to the bathroom and hurled her breakfast into the toilet.

The constant tick of the second hand of her wall clock usually calmed her. But right now it irked her. All things considered, the first full day of school with the entire student body went exceptionally well. Barbara Hardy had proven she fully deserved her title as "Super Secretary." After twenty years at the school, she knew every staff member, student—including his or her families—and where to find everything in the school.

Rotating her stiff neck in her hands, Meg smiled as she overheard Emma in the front office.

"Hi, Mrs. Hardy. Is the boss in?"

"Where else would she be? You Fulton girls work too much. Go on back. She's beat. Take her home and draw a nice warm bath."

"You should take your own advice, Mrs. Hardy." Emma smiled as she strolled into her mother's office. "Long day?"

"You could say that. I'll race you home, but I call shotgun on the tub," Meg said as she pulled her keys out of her purse.

"No can do. I'm pulling an all-nighter. Coach needs me to be at the game tonight. Shawn's wife started having contractions. Guess I'll be part of your staff for a few months."

Meg loved having her daughter work in the same school. A recent college graduate, Emma had a part time job as a physical therapist in town but continued looking for full-time work. When Meg heard the athletic trainer planned on taking some paternity time, she encouraged Emma to apply.

Now she wasn't so sure about the job. Emma volunteered in the afternoons, working with and learning the medical conditions of the high school athletes. Part of her job included getting to know the coaches as well and their practice and training procedures.

Which included befriending Coach McKay.

"Why don't you stick around for the football game tonight, Mom? This is your first school with a football program. You might even learn something," Emma teased.

"I'll pass. My bathtub and the bottle of chocolate wine I discovered at the store last week sound much more appealing." Meg kissed her daughter's cheek. "Have fun tonight. I'll wait up for you."

"I'm a big girl. No need to wait up. I'll probably head out to Martha's Pub with the coaches after the game. You should come."

"No thanks," Meg mumbled as she plastered on a fake smile.

The next few hours moved slowly. Too wound up to sleep and looking forward to "girl talk" with her daughter, Meg stayed awake, flipping through the channels. Not even Jimmy Kimmel could distract her sullen mood.

Waiting up for Emma brought back memories from her daughter's teenage years.

When Meg had started giving Emma a few more freedoms, the thick, hostile air between them slowly began to clear. There was no way she'd allow her sixteen-year-old to practice driving around the busy streets of Boston; much less get in a car with some of her newly licensed friends. Meg knew all too well about the evils that lurked in a teenager's car, which had led to many arguments with her daughter.

"You're so not fair! If I can't drive, I should be able to walk! What's the point of living in a city if you can't do anything but sit around all day and do homework?"

"The streets are dangerous, Emma. I need to know you're safe."

"Then can you drive me to the party? The basketball team just won the state—"

"No! No parties. I don't want you getting into trouble."

"Oh my God, Mom. Seriously! Can't you even trust me for a minute? I'm almost sixteen."

"You're a child. Stop trying to grow up so fast."

Six years later, the attitude had dropped, but the worry still lingered. Nothing would ever stop the worrying.

Headlights in the driveway jolted her mind back to the present. She wasn't waiting for her daughter to return from a friend's house—or a party. Thankfully Emma made it through high school without battle scars, unlike Meg.

Meg watched her daughter quietly open the door and flip on the living room light. Slipping out of her sneakers and dropping her keys inside the stinky shoes. Emma yawned and closed the front door behind her before she noticed Meg. "Mom, really. You didn't need to wait up." She plopped on the couch and rested her head on her mother's shoulder. Most would interpret the gesture as a sign that Emma was wiped and about to fall asleep. One of the quirks Meg loved about her daughter was her constant energy and her always-running mouth. Well, it wasn't *always* a good, but tonight it made Meg smile.

"You've got some decent kids in your school. I knew a few girls already from the field hockey camp this summer, but it's super cool to watch the way they play now. Awesome. Brings back memories." Emma jumped up and strolled into the kitchen. "Ice cream?"

"Sure," Meg said, following her. She took out two bowls out of the cabinet and placed them on the counter.

"And that football team. Wow. So freaking cool. Coach is amazing. The best. I'm in awe. The kids look up to him, and it seems like the coaches do too. You should see the way they work the sidelines, so focused and in tune with the game and their players. Not a single injury tonight. One really awesome tackle I figured for sure would have given Nick Mathers a concussion, but coach does so much conditioning. The team is really healthy. They didn't really even need me."

"You're spending too much time around teenagers. You're morphing back into one yourself," Meg teased.

Oh, her precious Emma. Never coming up for air, talking about every little detail of her day. Every personal encounter, every thought that entered her mind. How she ended up being the extrovert was beyond Meg's imagination. Emma definitely didn't inherit her social skills from her mother. The image of the father turned Meg's smile into a frown. *No, don't go there. She's nothing like him.*

"And. Oh. My. God, Mom." Emma held her hands up, palms out. "After the game, I went to Martha's with the coaches and a few teachers. You've got a totally cool staff, by the way. And coach…did I tell you how awesome he is on the field? Well, yeah in person he's laid back, funny, cool. Don't worry. I'm not going for the trophy wife image." She waved her spoon in the air. "He's totally old enough to be my dad. Well, maybe not that old. But anyway…" She stopped long enough to shovel a few oversized bites of ice cream down her throat.

Meg held her spoon midway to her mouth and gaped at her daughter.

"Kidding, Mom. Anyway, maybe you should ask him out. He's totally hot. I can give you the goods on him."

"The goods?"

"Yeah, like if he's single, married, divorced, a player. Stuff like that." Emma finished her ice cream, scraping the bowl for every last drop of mint chocolate chip. "I'm pretty sure he's single. Maybe divorced? Dunno." Emma scraped the bottom of her bowl and licked her spoon.

"I'm all set," she murmured and tossed her empty bowl in the sink.

Emma leaned against the counter and pouted. "What's the point of being in the same school if I can't give you the inside scoop?"

Meg shut the kitchen light off and searched for the remote in the living room. "And here I assumed you were excited about working in the same school as me because you loved me so much." She leaned down and kissed the top of Emma's head.

"I heard some talk about you today."

She knew where the conversation was headed, but Meg would not fall into the gossip mill. She didn't care what students or staff said about her. She fought to get to where she was, and no amount of gossip would pull her back to the deep dark hole that took her life away so many years ago.

"All good stuff," Emma said.

She didn't care what others said about her. Or so she told herself.

"Mostly about your clothes. Shoes. Hair."

"Emma, seriously, I don't care."

"Uh-huh. Then why do you dress like one of Tracy's customers? We're living in a hick-town. No need for high fashion here."

"I can't help if my best friend is a fashion consultant and I acquire tons of great clothes shipped to me on a regular basis. Besides, I have to look professional. I'm the principal."

Emma snorted. "Mom, have you noticed the way people dress around here? We're in New Hampshire. Three hours from Boston. The closest mall is forty-five minutes away. Flannel is the material of choice."

"You're exaggerating." Meg tried walking away from the conversation by turning off the television and heading upstairs, but her stubborn daughter tagged behind and continued prodding.

"Okay, so the flannel will probably come out in the winter, but the teachers are all casual. No suit and tie for the guys. I like it. They don't seem so stuffy."

Meg turned to her daughter. Emma's long, dark hair was identical to hers, but her those large, blue eyes mirrored someone else's. They were so beautiful, but also a haunting reminder of the past. They twinkled in a way that brought joyful memories.

So many feelings were expressed in those beautiful blue eyes. God blessed her daughter with a love of life.

"Yoo-hoo. Earth to Mom." Emma waved her hand in front of her mother's face.

Meg shook free from her thoughts, walked into her bathroom, and then squirted toothpaste on her toothbrush. "Hmm? What are you still bantering away on? Clothes, is it?"

"No, Mom. That was so five minutes ago. I asked you if you've talked with him yet."

"Who?"

"Coach. He totally looks like Bret Favre. But not in a

creepy, sexting way. The old Bret Favre. Well, the younger one before he got into his bit of trouble."

"Who? What?"

"Packers. Jets. Vikings. Sexting. He's got a little Tom Brady action going too. Forget it. You don't pay attention to football, but do you know the coach?"

"Coach?"

Sighing, Emma shook her head with growing impatience. "Now who sounds like the teenager? Are you even listening to me? McKay. Connor McKay. Have you met him yet? He's the head football and baseball coach but also teaches history. I realize you have a pretty big staff, and you've only been there a few weeks but he's kinda hard to forget."

Oh, that hot coach. Hot, arrogant, stubborn, and obstinate with amazing blue eyes and a body that could make her feel safe…or hunted. "Yeah, I met him." The last thing she needed was for her daughter to be in the middle of a stupid battle with a teacher. She turned away from her nosey daughter and brushed her teeth.

"Come on, Mom. Don't you think he's hot? It's been like forever since you've gone on a date, but you're not *that* old."

She raised an annoyed eyebrow. "*That* old? Gee, thanks. I'm not even forty and you're acting like I'm over the hill already. If you're done with your little interrogation of my clothing and lack of social life, I'm going to bed."

Some days, her mind and body seemed geriatric. And moments, rare moments, when she actually felt younger than her age. Ironically, it took her twenty-two-year-old daughter to make her feel young and vibrant.

It seemed like only yesterday Emma and Meg fought about everything, a volatile combination of puberty and denial. When Emma entered junior high, she had started her allure toward sports. Meg had fought her tooth and nail, steering her in the direction of drama, music, and art. Any subject but sports.

"You're so unfair, Mom. Why can't I try out for softball?" Emma's ponytail swayed with the sassy move of her head.

"You could get hurt, baby. Besides, softball won't get you anywhere in life. A good education will."

"Please. I'm twelve. I'm not quitting school, just picking up sports. I'm good, Mom. Mr. Faber asked me the other day in gym if I'd try out for his softball team. We're playing it in gym, and I'm wicked good."

"No. You need to keep your grades up and playing sports is going to interfere with what's important."

"I hate you! You want me to be like dumb, boring you! All you did was study in school and look how you turned out! You have no life and you're jealous of me and my friends!"

Emma hit the nail on the head with that argument. Once Meg backed off and allowed her daughter to grow up into her own person, they became extremely close. Sometimes Meg wondered if her role as mother was over. Lately, she felt more like her daughter's best friend. They were complete opposites but complimented each other beautifully and appreciated each other's differences. Too bad it wasn't that easy with all of her acquaintances.

Punching her pillow, Meg rolled over and tried to fall asleep, but she couldn't help mulling over her conversation with Connor McKay.

Touché.

What did he mean by that? She didn't personally attack the man, yet he sounded offended and almost defeated by something she said. Sure he tried to hide it, but she struck a nerve with him. He'd been completely bigheaded, smug, snobbish, and domineering in the three days since she first met him. Yet her daughter described him as funny, cool, laid back and…hot. Okay, she could secretly admit he was hot if she was into the chiseled, scruffy, strong type, which she wasn't, but he definitely was not laid back.

During every conversation she had with the man she could see the muscles in his jaw flex, his veins protrude from his very thick neck. Men like that used their physical strength to get what they wanted. And the fact he represented everything she despised, well that was the nail in his proverbial coffin. Hopefully their dislike for one another wouldn't affect Emma. If he treated her any differently because she was Meg's daughter, he'd have hell to pay.

Chapter Three

The first months of school went much better than expected. Athletes griped about being held accountable, but like Meg predicted, very few were benched. Instead, it seemed to be the motivating factor to stay on top of their studies. The after-school help sessions and study groups not only raised the athletes' grades, but other members of the student body also wanted to join in. The small handful of students who dropped off the teams had no desire to further their education and were directed toward the alternative education programs or given a tutor to help with their academic struggles. All in all, the administration and the staff at NHS continued to work extremely hard with all students, not just the athletes. The morale among the teachers slowly improved once they realized they too received the support they needed to meet the needs of their students.

The school wasn't so large that she could prevent running into Connor McKay, but she did her best to avoid him. They had not spoken a word to each other since the incident in the conference room unless they were in front of dozens of other teachers. His football team had been playing well, so he had nothing to complain about—or so she hoped. Meg figured as soon as they lost a game he'd come storming into her office, blaming the season's first loss on her, but it never happened.

Shawn, the school's Athletic Director, had asked to work part-time for the remainder of the school year. His newborn son had complications from a heart defect and he needed to dedicate his time to his family. Emma was a shoe-in for the AD position, but Meg needed to go through the correct procedures. The superintendent and the school board asked for an official evaluation of Emma before they would type up a formal contract, not only from the coaches but from Meg as well. They trusted her to keep her personal attachment aside and write up a fair evaluation, which required her to interview the coaches Emma worked with.

Including Connor McKay.

Avoiding conversation with him had allowed the school year to run smoothly, but she had procrastinated as much as possible; the report was due in the morning. And, of course, it was parent-teacher conference night. Parents filled most of Connor's slots—being the most popular teacher—so she had to settle for the last appointment of the night.

Meg showed up outside Connor's door promptly at ten minutes to nine, clutching a clipboard to her chest. Not a second earlier—no need in adding to their lengthy ten minutes—but not wanting to be late. She smoothed her hand down her black turtleneck sweater and picked imaginary lint off her gray slacks.

Nine o'clock rolled around, and he was still talking with the same set of parents. She toyed with the idea of leaving, claiming she needed to head home, but the conference was for Emma.

Meg smiled politely as the parents exited the room. Connor shuffled papers around on his desk and looked up at Meg.

"Sorry, we ran over. You can leave if it's too late," Connor said, turning his back and packing up his school bag.

How dare he excuse her after she had been waiting for him for—she looked up at the clock in his room—twenty minutes!

"Excuse me, but Emma deserves to hear what the coaches have to say about her progress so far. If she has made such little impact on you and your athletes, and you have absolutely nothing constructive to say about her, I'll be sure to pass the information along." Meg turned on her three-inch designer black boots and took a step toward the door.

"Whatever, leave…wait…come back. Sit down." He sighed and sat on top of a desk in the front row.

Meg turned around and crossed her arms, using the clipboard as a shield, thankful he hadn't called her bluff. Emma *really* needed his recommendation. "Gee, Mr. McKay, I'm not seeing the laid back, funny guy Emma has been telling me about. You sound like a complete jackass." The words came rolling out of her mouth so fast she had no time to take them back.

Connor smirked. "I had that coming. I can see where Emma gets her mouth."

"She's called you a jackass too?"

Connor tipped his head back and laughed. "No, but she definitely says what she thinks. No holds barred for that one."

Meg tentatively sat at the edge of one of the student desks, leaving an empty row between her and Connor. "She doesn't…she doesn't cross the line, does she?"

"Emma? No. She's great with the kids. Really sensitive to their aches and pains. She listens but doesn't coddle them. Loves to debate with the coaches on how far to push the kids. She may be totally wrong or have a completely off-base opinion, but she's not afraid to say it.

I like that about her."

"And she's doing her job well?"

He nodded. "The best. You'd never know she had less than a year's experience under her belt. She's a good athlete too. She practices right along with the kids, watching their form and coaching them on how to support their ankle, knee, or whatever body part needs protection. I do have one problem with her though."

Meg stopped writing on her clipboard and contemplated telling him off. "Yes?"

"She's young. Attractive. My boys get pretty distracted when she's around." He smirked.

"So you're discriminating against my…Emma because of her appearance?" Meg raised an eyebrow and pretended to scribble notes on her pad.

"Easy. That's not what I meant. She does her job well. I have no problem recommending her as a fill-in while Shawn is out. But maybe she could cover up a little more. You know, longer shorts, looser shirt? It's a matter of dress code, that's all."

"I do believe that's a very sexist comment," she growled under her breath. *And completely off base.* If there was anyone who could care less what she wore, it was Emma. Her outfit of choice consisted of a pair of warm-up pants and sweatshirt in the winter and shorts and grubby T-shirts in the summer.

"No. It's practical. She's working with teenagers who drip more hormones than our leaky faucet in the faculty lounge. Maybe she could borrow something out of your closet. You two look to be about the same size and shape. You're always buttoned up." He turned to his desk and picked up his keys.

"Mr. McKay you're digging your hole deeper and deeper. You continue these sexist remarks about Emma and myself and I *will* write you up. Your feelings toward me will have no bearing on—"

"You asked for my opinion and I gave it. I thought you figured that out about me." He walked toward the door and gestured for her to leave the classroom.

"You're a—"

"Easy now." He held up a finger to quiet her. "Don't start making false accusations. I may be stubborn, but I'm honest. I didn't realize she was your daughter until recently. We're on a first-name basis."

"And had you known earlier, you would have fed her to the wolves?"

"I think I would have hit the ground running."

"Meaning?"

"You scare the hell out of me, Ms. Fulton." He smiled, but it didn't reach his eyes.

Was he teasing her? Complimenting her? Insulting her?

"I can say likewise, Mr. McKay."

He laughed again. Twice in one night. She'd known him for three months, and it took a five-minute conversation to finally see the human side of Connor McKay.

"You and I definitely have our differences, but I'm not too stubborn to admit when someone else is right."

"And you're wrong?"

"No," he laughed. "I'm not admitting I'm wrong. But can admit when I'm beat. Your daughter is a strong, amazing young woman. I can see where she inherited her strength. You and I may not coach the same way, but we play for the same team. Emma Fulton will be a valuable asset to our team as well."

The flood of compliments and change in attitude confused Meg. Was he playing her for a fool, or did he really respect her?

The little dimple in his chin and laugh lines around his eyes softened his rough exterior. His blue eyes lit up when he laughed.

"Not a trusting kind, are you?"

Damn. Emma's description had been spot on. He was hot. Not that she cared. His smile brought chills down her arms and little flutters to her stomach. A sensation she never experienced before. He was the type of man who flashed a smile, flexed his arms, and got away with whatever he wanted.

The kind of man who could hurt her.

Meg quickly stood and said, "Well then, if you have any concerns regarding Emma's work, you know how to contact me."

She stormed out of his classroom and did not turn back. Once upon a time his type played her, but she had since prepared herself and would not fall ignorant to an athlete's alluring eyes and sexy laugh.

No. Never, ever again.

Chapter Four

Other than the usual disgruntled parent, the handful of frequent school skippers and the occasional cigarette smoked in the boy's bathroom, Meg's professional life ran rather smoothly. Since Connor's glowing recommendation for Emma, they'd had few encounters but smiled politely at each other when passing in the hall. Her personal life, not that she'd consider Connor a part of it, remained dormant and for the first time, Meg allowed her mind to wander to the opposite sex.

Or rather, to Connor McKay. She couldn't deny her physical attraction to him, but she'd be damned before she ever did anything about it. Juggling her laptop and a hot cup of Dunkin Donuts pumpkin coffee in her right hand and moving a stack of file folders and binders under her left arm, Meg shimmied the keys to her office door and let herself in without missing a beat. She dropped the files on her desk and took a rewarding sip from the warm Styrofoam cup.

"Heaven," she murmured into the steam.

She opened up her laptop and scrolled through her e-mails, deleting Spam mail, forwarding messages to the appropriate people, and marking others as "urgent." Expecting to forward the e-mail from the football commission to Emma, the interim Athletic Director, Meg quickly scanned through the message and froze.

*The New Hampshire Athlete Association is happy to announce Connor McKay's nomination as this year's Football Coach of the Year. As his principal, you are cordially invited...*Meg raced through the e-mail. As his principal, Meg had to inform him of the honor and attend the banquet with him in a few weeks. She gazed out her window at the fall landscape. New England's chilly nights turned the leaves bright orange, red, and yellow, while the windy days continued to strip the glorious statues of their natural beauty, littering the ground with piles of tricolored leaves, dry and crisp from the cool air.

Funny how her mood mirrored the seasons. In September she had been bright, cheerful, and optimistic. Now the near-barren November trees, dead earth, and chilly days reflected how empty and alone she felt. Emma had no trouble at all fitting in and making new friends. Her most recent inseparable pal was Paige Thorne. Fitting that Annie Thorne, Paige's mother and English teacher at the high school, and Meg formed a friendship as well. Her family owned a horse farm and Emma had taken up riding. She was a natural. It could often be a challenge squeezing in lessons between her morning hours as a physical therapist and afternoons as a substitute athletic director, but if anyone could do it, Emma could.

It pleased Meg that, like a chameleon, her daughter could adapt to almost any culture, any situation, and had a plethora of friendships. Emma had the kind of life Meg had always dreamed about: fun and carefree. For the past twenty-two years, she focused first on being a young—very young—mother, and as her daughter grew and matured, Meg worked on establishing her career. Now she had both—career and grown daughter. It was time to make a life for herself.

Slowly, very slowly, Meg started forming friendships. Annie Thorne had proven herself to be an excellent teacher and a caring woman. Quite regularly, she invited Meg to Martha's, where most teachers hung out on Friday afternoons, and just as regularly Meg declined. They talked a lot at school and ate lunch together, but she had yet to take Annie up on an offer to go out. It was her fault for feeling so alone. She needed to find a life outside her daughter and her job. But living in small town America made it nearly impossible.

Annie was great, but Meg didn't feel comfortable calling her up out of the blue and asking her to hang out. And her past still loomed over her. Not a bombshell she wanted to dump on a newfound friendship. When she felt really alone or needed someone to talk to, she could always pick up the phone and call Tracy, but she needed someone here, not in New York.

Reading the invitation to the banquet, Meg groaned. Social settings were not her forte`. She had no practice. And alone with Connor? And in Manchester? No way. She would find an excuse to bail out of it. Maybe ask another teacher to go in her place. Maybe Jim, the assistant principal, would go. That could work.

Meg left her office and walked the five steps to Jim's office and knocked lightly on his door. "Have a minute?"

"Sure, come in." His yellow shirt had a coffee stain by his pocket, which overflowed with various pens and pencils. He pushed his oversized glasses up his nose and gestured toward one of the chairs next to his cluttered desk. "This doesn't look to good. What's wrong?"

Always perceptive, except when it came to his own appearance. "Oh, it's nothing really." She tucked her skirt under her legs as she sat at the edge of the chair. "I just received an e-mail about Coach McKay." She summarized the e-mail for him. "And since you have known Connor a lot longer than I have, I figured you might like to go."

Jim scratched his balding head and looked down at his desk calendar. "Darn, I'd love to go, but it's our twenty-fifth anniversary. Carol will skin me alive if I stand her up." Leaning back in his worn desk chair, he toyed with a pen in his pocket. "You'll have fun. Never met a girl who didn't have a good time with McKay."

Meg took a sharp breath and stared wide-eyed at her usual docile assistant principal.

Catching on to what he said, he leaned forward and stuttered. "Oh, darn, Meg. I didn't mean it like that. Oh shoot." Jim stood and paced, avoiding eye contact. "I'm sorry. Darn-it-all. I just meant…uh, well, everyone loves Connor. Guys too." He blushed. "I mean, well, I didn't mean. I meant—"

"It's okay, Jim. I get it. Connor's a great guy. Funny. Everyone wants to be his friend." She said it all mockingly, but Jim, caught up in his own embarrassment, didn't pick up on her sarcasm. "I'll have a grand ol' time."

Leaving his office, she felt worse than she did five minutes ago. Cloudy images of That Night twenty-three years ago played like a horror flick through her mind. Her body shook as she made a failing attempt to warm herself by hugging her shaking hands around her middle. Fear took over her body as she made her way back to her office. Closing the door behind her, Meg slowed her rapid breathing and practiced her meditation routine. Eyes closed, shoulders relaxed, breathe in…one…two…three, breathe out…one…two…three. Concentrating on clearing her mind, Meg imagined a slowly running stream flowing through her limbs and releasing all her stress and tension out of her hands and feet.

She wouldn't allow the fear to enter her body. She was strong, capable, and no one's fool. A stupid awards banquet filled with idiotic jocks wouldn't knock her down.

Reluctantly, Meg opened her eyes, powered up her laptop, and added one more item to tomorrow's faculty meeting agenda.

Chapter Five

"You really don't have to drive me. I can meet you there." Meg straightened her blouse and stood ramrod straight in the doorway of Connor's classroom, not wanting to completely enter his territory the same way he evaded being fully in her office. He spent a lot of time in the main office, flirting with Barbara, talking with other teachers, picking up his mail, and avoiding Meg. As head of the history department, he had to meet with her monthly, but there was safety in numbers there. She followed his cue and kept her distance as well. Unfortunately there was no way to avoid him tonight.

"Manchester is a two hour drive. No sense in us both driving. I'll pick you up a little before five."

"Since you're the 'Man of the Hour,'" she quoted with her fingers, "shouldn't I be driving you?" In her car, she could be in control. In his car…no, she would not think about *that*.

"Call me sexist if you must, but I'll drive."

Yeah, she'd call him sexist. Taking a cleansing breath and willing herself to be strong, Meg rolled her eyes and gave him directions to her house. He didn't write them down and told her he'd pick her up her in two hours. Yikes. Two hours. She quickly left his room and returned to her office. The invitation said semiformal. Thank God she had Tracy's endless supply of cocktail dresses filling her closet, still with their tags on.

The pile of paperwork on her desk made a nice distraction. No need to rush home. It wasn't a date, far from it. She didn't care what she looked like. Connor represented the enemy to whom she must be civil, but definitely not worth spending two hours in front of the mirror for. She would be in control. Or at least she hoped.

Emma had different plans than her laid-back mother. Giddy over the idea of her mother going out with the hottest teacher, hell the hottest man she ever met, Emma brainstormed ways to make the night unforgettable. Never in her twenty-two years had she ever recalled her mother being out on a date. And while this wasn't a *date* date, it was a date for her mom. Coach McKay, single and *hunkalicious*; Meg Fulton single and beautiful. Why not work on her matchmaking skills?

A little past three, her mom finally made it back to the office. Emma paced impatiently. "Mom! I almost had Barbara page you on your walkie-talkie."

Meg rushed over and placed her hands on Emma's face. "Why? What's wrong? Are you okay?"

She pushed her mother's hands away. "I'm fine, Mom, but you need to hurry home and get ready for tonight."

"Oh, tonight is the big awards banquet!" Barbara chimed in. "I hope our Connor receives the recognition he deserves. He's done so much for our community since he returned."

Meg opened her mouth to ask her secretary a question, but Emma interrupted, "Come on Mom, I've got your keys. Let's go." She had hair and makeup, and a lot of convincing to do. She saw the simple short-sleeved, floor-length gown her mother picked out for tonight. Emma knew her mother preferred simple and classy, but it wasn't the image she needed to *wow* McKay.

Thankfully, her mother had agreed to carpool today and Emma could usher her out of school at a decent hour. They drove in silence. Not wanting to push her mother too much, Emma actually stayed quiet while delicious plans of sexing her mother up ran circles in her head.

Emma put the car in Park and turned off the ignition. "You hit the shower, and I'll make us a snack and help you pick out your clothes."

"I already have my outfit," Meg said as she got out of the car and walked toward the front door.

"Uh-huh." Emma nodded, followed her mother inside the house, and then shooed her mother into the shower. When she entered her mother's room, she went to the closet and pulled out two dresses. A decoy and the winner. Looking around the bedroom, she frowned at the plain and boring white on white decor. If it weren't for Tracy, her mother's wardrobe would be the same monochromatic scheme.

Minutes later her mother stepped out of the shower, wrapped in her favorite emerald green silk robe—compliments of Tracy and Saks—hair bundled in a towel on top of her head. She stopped abruptly when she saw the dresses Emma laid out for her.

"Honey, I told you I already picked out my dress." She went to the closet and pulled out the long, black, old lady dress.

"Yeah, Mom, about that. I don't think it's the dress for tonight. It's more…I dunno, like an old bridesmaid dress."

"Em, it's Donna Karan."

"Yeah, whatever. It still isn't right for tonight."

"It's a football awards banquet. What do you expect me to wear? A cheerleading outfit?"

Emma smiled. "No, not exactly, but something more fun. I say the red." She held up the decoy, a short, tight fitted red dress that revealed too much cleavage, not that her mom had much to show.

"There's a reason the tag is still on that one. Just because Tracy sends me the dress, doesn't mean I have to wear it. Like you said before, we're in New Hampshire, not Boston. Or New York."

"Okay, then how about the sage?" Emma held her real pick against her body, which was only two inches shorter than her mother's five eight frame, and wiggled her eyebrows. "It says fun, hip, sexy yet conservative."

The Badgley Mischka one-shoulder dress gathered on the right and had a flutter sleeve, giving her right arm a little coverage. The skirt, skimming slightly above the knee, would show off her mother's thin and toned legs.

"Don't you think it's a bit much for tonight?"

"Much? Nah, it's perfect. And wear your hair down."

"Down?"

"Yeah, you wear it up all week. Let it down and relax tonight."

Meg walked back into her bathroom and began drying her hair. Emma smiled quite smugly. While her mother knew how to dress for work, she definitely had no idea how to dress for a man. Her hair was one of her best assets, and her mother needed to learn how to work it. She held some back with a clip, in a tight bun or pulled it all back in a twist to keep it out of her face while working. All the pictures of stars in *People* and *US Weekly* showed gorgeous manes of hair. It was the hot look. Her mom needed to be hot tonight as well.

Her mom had been playing it cool, as if she didn't consider tonight a big deal, but the signs were so obvious. Two days ago she had her eyebrows waxed.

Again. It had only been a little over two weeks since her last visit to the salon. She painted her toes. Again. While she typically kept her toes and hands perfectly manicured, she never redid them in the same week. "Wrong shade," her mother said when Emma had walked in on her taking her perfect polish off last night.

Emma had to smile. Maybe her mom didn't have the hots for McKay, but it was her first date in…ever. A little while later, her mom came down the stairs barefoot holding two different pair of shoes.

"Okay, fashion expert. Not that it matters, but since you're going to criticize whatever I wear, I might as well ask for your opinion. Are these shoes okay?" She held up a pair of black, open toe, closed back heels. Nice but she wore them to work regularly.

"As if." Emma rolled her eyes. "Sexy shoes, Mom. Go for the gold open-toe, open back, strappy three-inch heels. You never wear those."

"Em, I don't want to go for sexy. This isn't a date. It's a banquet with a bunch of…coaches." She shuddered.

The doorbell rang and she ran back up the stairs. Emma smiled at her mother's retreating back, opened the door, and froze. Her jaw dropped as she stared at the coach. McKay looked totally hot wearing his usual khakis and polo shirts or athletic gear on the field, but hot damn, throw him in a suit and…wow!

"McKay. You clean up real nice." She backed away so he could enter the house.

He smirked at her and tugged at his tie. "Thanks. God, I hate wearing these things."

"Come on in. Mom's just finishing up." She led him to the small living room and plopped herself on the end of the couch. He remained standing and looked around the living room.

"Cozy."

"Yup. Just us girls." Emma was tempted to say more but didn't want to embarrass him. Embarrass her mom she could do, but not the coach. She whistled when she saw her mom come down the stairs. The dress and the shoes complimented her figure and long legs. Her mom was beautiful. She sneaked a peek at McKay and saw the change in his face. His usual smirk and dimple were gone, replaced by a serious, almost scowling face.

This had to be good, right?

Well, holy shit. The woman always looked fine and well put together, even out on the field when she had to attend the games, her jeans were stylish, the sweaters, sneakers…always looked good. But tonight, damn, tonight she was incredible. Sexy. Edible. He wanted to lick his way up her neck and plunge his hands in her mass of dark, wavy hair. He didn't trust himself to speak, so he simply stared. And fantasized.

The whistle behind him reminded him he was also in the company of Emma, Meg's daughter nonetheless, and the images running through his head were definitely not suitable for a younger audience. He turned and smiled at Emma, "Well, kid. I'll make sure to have your mom home by curfew. Stay out of trouble." He walked to the front door and opened it for Meg. "After you." He gestured with his hand.

Meg walked over to Emma and bent down to kiss her on the forehead. "Call me if you need me, sweetie." She sauntered through the front door without so much as a quick glance or word to Connor.

She was nervous. He could handle that. But, damn, her dress only covered one of her arms, baring her delicious, soft, satin skin on the left. That, he could not handle. He swallowed and cleared his throat as he followed her citrus scent down the short walkway to his car. Like a true gentleman, he opened the car door for her and closed it lightly after watching her tuck her long, sculpted legs into the car.

Rounding the hood of his black Audi Spyder, he tugged at his tie again and tried to recall some of the "safe" conversation topics he could bring up during their two-hour drive. He positioned himself in the driver's seat, put the car in reverse, and, out of habit, stretched his right arm across the back of the passenger's seat as he backed out of the driveway. The jump Meg made did not escape his notice. She was rigid as she stared out the front window, hands clutching a slim purse. Her left naked shoulder taunting him in the moonlight.

When they were on the road and his hands were safely back on the steering wheel, her shoulders relaxed. A little.

"Uh, you look nice." It sounded corny, but he couldn't remember if he complimented her yet.

"Thanks."

"Sure."

The awkward silence hung thick in the air. Connor didn't really want to talk about himself, and he figured the banquet would be a safe topic to discuss.

"Should be a lot of people there tonight."

"Yeah."

Okay, so that didn't instigate thrilling conversation, but he didn't actually say anything insightful. Maybe if he asked her a question.

"How was your day?" Again. Lame.

"Fine."

She wasn't making the car ride easy and there was no way he could endure one hour and fifty more minutes of hostile silence. He didn't even want to go to the damn banquet anyway, not after the last one. There were a million reasons why he didn't invite his coaching staff, players, or any of his family to tag along. The night was sure to be living hell. When Meg announced his nomination at the faculty meeting, the staff applauded and were positive this time would be different. Connor, however, wasn't about to take any chances. No point in putting the people he cared about through the insults and drama. Meg already thought low of him so he honestly didn't mind her witnessing an escapade. Still, the silent treatment was killing him. He'd rather argue than listen to the quiet hostility.

"Okay, Meg. Cards on the table." He quickly glanced at her and then moved his gaze back to the road. "We had a rocky start. Not all of it was your fault—"

"*My* fault?" She turned in her seat, her chocolate brown eyes shooting daggers into his side. He tried not to let his gaze roam down her thigh, but he couldn't help it if her dress slid up, revealing legs longer than his record-breaking 101-yard touchdown run in the divisional playoffs against the Giants. "I'm just doing my job, and a damn good job of it if I do say so myself, and you pick a fight over everything I do, every decision I make, and every change I suggest. You obviously have a problem with a woman in power and you hate the fact that I'm right in all our disagreements. So don't try to make it look like you're taking the high road by claiming our issues are fifty-fifty."

Whoa. He stayed silent while processing what she said. Their first altercation was about the athletic eligibility program. Okay, he'd admit the program worked. Being benched for the weekend game had been the perfect carrot to dangle in front of his academically unmotivated athletes. Their second big argument happened in October during homecoming. He gave his football team permission to spray paint the road leading to the school.

"Absolutely not!"

"It's tradition around here."

Meg folded her arms across her chest. "Homecoming traditions are one thing. Trash-talking graffiti on the main road leading to the High School is inappropriate and disrespectful."

Connor scowled at her. "My team has worked their asses off. They're undefeated and playing their rival, the

Hornets, this weekend. And I'm not talking about trash talking. All the kids want to do is show some school spirit."

"And what happens when they accidentally spray something inappropriate?"

"The other coaches and I will monitor them."

She sighed, "Chalk. No spray paint. And you and your coaching staff must be present the entire time."

"Chalk? Are you friggin' kidding me? They're not toddlers. Spray paint. Nothing will go wrong."

"Chalk. And I doubt that."

The road looked great when the team went home that night. Unfortunately, some kids came back in the middle of the night and sprayed comments like, *We'll sting your ass! You suck and then you die.* While none of the sayings contained racist or vulgar comments, they were inappropriate. He was angry Meg had been right, but he didn't apologize. Instead, he'd reamed his team out after the game and made them run an extra two miles before practice on Monday afternoon, but now felt guilty about not listening or apologizing to Meg.

"Sorry about Homecoming. Things did get a little out of hand."

"*Out of hand*?"

Thankfully, she turned back around and stared, seethed rather, out her window. Unfortunately, she pulled the bottom of her dress down so it covered her thighs. While he missed the golden flesh, he was grateful she took away the distraction.

"The chalk talk was a good idea. We could've washed off the crap the kids wrote after I left."

She didn't say a word.

"I hung out for three hours watching those kids. You have to admit, the pictures and sayings the team came up with were pretty creative. *The Hornets.*" He chuckled. "Laskey set themselves up for ridicule when they made annoying little insects their mascot." Still silence. "So that's not why you're pissed at me? Is it the comment I made about you needing to get out more?"

"*Get out more*?"

Shit. "I guess you didn't hear that one."

He rubbed his hand across his face, pinching the bridge of his nose. The silence was better than her repeating everything he said and him sticking his foot in his mouth. After too many uncomfortable minutes he brought out the charm.

"Have I told you how beautiful you look tonight?"

She snorted. *Snorted.* The beautiful, in control, respected principal and mother, snorted. Liking the more human side of Meg, he tried another tactic. Women liked to be complimented on their age.

"You definitely look too young to have a twenty-something old daughter." He turned and flashed her his million dollar smile that sold a ton of airtime on ESPN. Ouch. If looks could kill. The glare radiating from her face nearly made his testicles retract. Where had he gone wrong? For the first time, an attractive woman was not susceptible to any of his charm. Not that it oozed out of him tonight. But what he said was true. The parents of high school students he encountered didn't look anything like her.

Forget trying. Kissing her ass didn't work. And while it was an excellent ass, he never stooped so low before, so why bother now? If she hated him, so be it. They were heading to a football banquet. His turf. He'd suffer in silence for—he glanced at the clock—another hour and twenty-two minutes. Connor turned the music up and pressed his foot down farther. Maybe if he drove a little faster he could make it without wringing her slender, naked neck.

Meg glanced over at the speedometer. Ninety. Twenty-five miles over the speed limit. She wanted to get the dreadful car ride and stupid banquet over and done with but also wanted to avoid an accident.

"In a hurry?"

He didn't hear her. How could he with the music blaring so loud? Thirty minutes into the drive, after an ill attempt at making conversation and finding nothing on the radio, he put in a Guns N' Roses CD and turned it up to a decimating volume. The last place on Earth she wanted to be was trapped in a room with hundreds of other athletes. It did strike her odd why Connor didn't want to bring any friends, family, or coaching staff, but what did she know about the stranger sitting next to her? He probably spawned himself from a test tube mixing the perfect amount of testosterone, athletic ability, physical appearance, intelligence, and arrogance.

The alpha male. Too good for family. Too self-centered for real friends. Not that she cared. Meg Fulton was just as good. Better. Mother, principal, independent, smart, and stylish. She played with the silver bracelet on her left wrist. *Was that it?* Did she have as little substance as Connor? God, she was just as bad as Mr. Arrogance sitting to her left. Risking her pride, but determined to erase the "bitch status" she gained if not in the past few months, definitely in the past hour, she reached to the control panel and turned down the music.

"Too loud? I figured after raising a teenager and being surrounded by teens all day, you'd be used to it." Connor ejected the CD and changed the station to an easy listening station.

"I believe we'll still make it in time if you drive the speed limit."

Connor noticed the speedometer and eased up on the gas. "G N' R has that effect on me."

"Nice car. I'll have to review the salary scale. We're

obviously overpaying our staff." She meant the sarcasm to come off lightheartedly, but his tense jaw told her otherwise.

They drove in silence again. Meg really wanted to end the awkwardness. It wasn't fair to compare Connor to…*him*.

"Is this the first time you've been nominated?"

He glanced at her quickly. "No."

"Have you ever won?"

"No."

Ah, a little role reversal. He seemed to be playing her game. Meg rolled her eyes and played the part of the better person. "Sorry. Maybe this is your year. Your team obviously respects you and played very well and you had a good season, despite some of the obstacles set before you."

"Mmm."

"Do you have an acceptance speech prepared?"

"No."

"When were you nominated before?"

"Few years ago."

She sat fuming. She tried. What did he expect? Meg figured she had two choices. Stop trying or end the game.

Twisting in her seat, she faced Connor, sucked in a deep breath, and sighed. "I'm sorry for being a bitch." She wasn't letting him off the hook by turning back in her seat. Instead, she stared at his profile and waited for a response.

It didn't take long. The sexy grin Emma raved about for weeks made its way to his eyes and deep into her gut. The dimple in his chin became even more pronounced as the grin grew into a full-fledged smile.

"Forgiven. Sorry about being a stubborn bastard."

"Hmm, you realize sorry means you won't do it again."

"Well, in that case, I take part of it back. I'm sorry

about being a bastard. The stubborn part you're going to have to live with."

"I accept." She turned again in her seat and lost her smile as she took in the view. As they neared Manchester, the lights from neighboring cities lit up the interior of the car. The city hosted closets full of secrets and skeletons. The advice Tracy gave her earlier today on the phone went out the window as soon as they crossed the Merrimack River.

"It was a long time ago, Meg. You're different. Emma tells me this Connor guy is one of the good ones. You have to let yourself live a little."

Flashbacks of fear, confusion, and pain filled her head. Her heart raced and palms began to sweat. She hadn't been to Manchester in over twenty years and had no plans of ever returning. The past was behind her and she'd moved on, making a life for her and Emma. Still, the pain from so long ago flooded through her veins as they drove through the city. Practicing her meditation, Meg slowed her breathing and unclenched her hands, watching as the little half-moon impressions her perfectly manicured fingernails made in her palms began to fade. *Calm your breathing. Pretend everything is normal.*

"So, will this be some stuffy banquet lasting all night or do we eat, accept the award, and leave?"

"Confident I'll win are you?"

"No, hungry."

He chuckled. "I hate to say it, but you'll probably be the center of attention tonight." Her stomach, weak with unfamiliar fluttering, turned into a nervous brick.

"Why do you say that?"

"Well, there aren't many female football coaches. Well, any really. There will be a few wives tonight, but mostly it's a guy night."

"And you're telling me this now? I wouldn't have come. I asked Jim to, but it's his anniversary tonight."

He smiled. “Spending the evening with a beautiful woman will lessen the blow if I don’t win.”

“Oh, please. Feed me another line. I’m here as your principal, not your date. You could have brought one, you know.”

“Yeah, I know.”

They drove in companionable silence until the god-awful music started to repeat itself. Meg’s nerves had finally simmered but started churning again when Connor pulled off the turnpike and into the parking lot of the hotel. “Would you like me to drop you off while I park the car? The lot is pretty full. And you didn’t bring a coat.”

Connor’s presence in her living room, dressed to the nines, heated her so much she actually forgot to bring her coat. Meg’s uneasiness weighed more heavily as she noticed the men wearing suits socializing outside the hotel. “No, I can walk. I like the fresh air.” She clutched her purse until her knuckles turned white and concentrated on her breathing as he maneuvered his sleek vehicle into a parking spot, not missing the irony in feeling safer by Connor’s side.

Playing the role of the gentleman tonight, he opened her door and held out his hand to help her out of the low-slung car. His hand, warm and calloused, felt surprisingly comforting. Since when had being with Connor felt safe? He turned from enemy to protector in a matter of minutes. She didn’t recognize anyone at the banquet so she stayed close to Connor’s side, not wanting to be left alone. Meg didn’t resist when he put his hand on the small of her back and led her into the hotel. The simple, light touches brought back the fluttering to her stomach, which did well to offset the anchor buried deep in her belly. Holding her head high and her rolling her shoulders back, she plastered on a polite smile as Connor talked with his friends. An elderly man came rushing over to him and pat him hard on the back.

"Good luck, Connor. Damn fine season. This time will be different."

Connor tensed for a second, then added, "We'll see, Greg. Tim Jacoby and Ryan Levers had outstanding seasons this year as well."

"Don't be so modest. You're the best guy out there."

He ignored the compliment. "Greg, this is Meg Fulton. Meg, Greg Randolph. He was my peewee football coach back in the day."

"And always finds the best ladies too." Greg picked up Meg's hand and kissed it as if she were royalty. Without taking his smiling gaze off her, he spoke to Connor, "What the hell does this fine lady see in the likes of you? Run away with me, Meg. I cook a fine breakfast and will treat you better than this old boy."

Connor laughed. "How's Marie? Did she come tonight?"

"Like she'd miss a chance to hang out with her favorite boy. We found seats at your table." He winked and looped his arm through Meg's, leading her to one of the tables up front. He was stronger than he looked and fit the part of the flirty old man quite well. She liked him instantly. "Connor here is like the son we never had. Four girls. Tried to marry one off on Connor, but the good-for-nothing' chump thought he was too good for her."

Meg scowled at Connor.

"His youngest, Janie is eight years older than me," he whispered in her ear. The soft air from his mouth and light brush of his lips sent shockwaves of goosebumps down her arms. The fresh scent of soap and something unfamiliar—man?—filled the air.

"But here I am carrying on like he's the man of the hour when really I want to know more about the lovely angel on my arm." Greg patted her hand and beamed friendly brown eyes down at her.

Before she had time to utter a word, a woman who

appeared to be in her late sixties stood and wrapped Connor in a bear hug. He lifted her off her feet and kissed her smack on the lips.

"Why Marie, you haven't changed a bit. Still kiss like the goddess you are."

"Ah, sugar, we missed you. How's your family?"

So he did have a family. And he was becoming more human by the minute. Connor pulled out a chair for Marie and then gestured to Meg to sit next to her. He placed himself to her left and she felt his gaze linger on her bare shoulder.

"Great. Mom and Pop are hoping to retire soon, but I can't imagine that happening."

"Send them my love, will you? We don't make our way up to Newhall enough. Sure do miss everyone." Marie smiled affectionately at Greg in a loving, knowing manner, a moment Meg hoped she'd be able to share someday with a husband. If she could ever get over her fear of being alone with a man. "Now, listen to me gibbering on. No manners to speak of. I'm Marie." She stretched out her arms and hugged Meg.

"Nice to meet you, Marie. I'm Meg."

"And how did you come across my sugar here?" Marie winked at Connor. "A fine catch he is."

"No, it's not like that. He is…uh, I'm his…I'm the principal at Newhall High."

"Ah," Greg said, winking at Connor. "Going for the boss, eh?"

"No! I mean, no, I came tonight as a representative from the school. We're not…I'm not…it's only business."

"Sure, dear," Greg said as he patted Meg's hand. "Just a business meeting." He kissed his wife on her cheek and sat down on the other side of her.

Meg looked to Connor for backup, but he sat silently sipping his beer. Grinning of course, his simple, sexy little grin that offset his laugh lines and made his baby blues twinkle. She picked up her wineglass, which magically appeared while she was talking with Marie, and sipped away her dignity.

Dinner was probably delicious, but Meg had been too nervous to taste the food. Small talk at the table brought many laughs and heartwarming smiles. The Randolphs had fond memories of Connor in peewee football and high school days. When they started to talk about his college career, Connor cut them off and changed the subject to his current high school team. When his previous nomination came up, he did the same. There were pieces of his past he obviously didn't want Meg to hear. Why, she wasn't sure, and it only made her more curious. The Randolphs picked up on the unspoken message and followed along Connor's guidelines keeping the conversation light and flowing.

"And what about you, dear? Where are you from?"

Meg took another sip of water and played with her strawberry shortcake. "The Boston area." No need to mention she grew up in Manchester. She cut all her ties to the city years ago, and she had no desire to ever mend them.

"And what is your family like?"

"My parents died when I was young. It's just my grandparents and my daughter," she said softly and then excused herself to the ladies' room.

Her short reply and abrupt departure to the restroom made it clear she'd like to keep her personal life private. Meg stared at her reflection in the bathroom mirror. Confused and overwhelmed at her reaction to Connor, she splashed water on her face and blotted it dry with a paper towel, hoping to wash away the unwelcome flutters in her belly every time he touched her. Every time he looked at her with those amazing blue eyes.

Thankfully no one at the table asked any more personal questions when she returned.

After a slide show of the three nominees—which

bellowed a heartwarming Kenny Chesney song—and speeches made by television and newspaper journalists who followed the coaches and teams, the coach of the year award was given to Connor McKay. He stood modestly and smiled. Marie kissed him on the cheek and Greg gave him a hug. He turned to Meg and she stared back, nervous he might kiss her, nervous he might not.

Instead, he turned and stepped up to the podium to accept his award. After the typical thank you to his assistant coaches and exemplary players, he added one final thought.

"This year my buttons got pushed when someone showed me it's not only about the game but about molding and sculpting individuals into life-long learners. It's about teaching them the skills so they can fight, work, and play on their own. So they have a chance at a future."

She didn't hear the rest of his speech. Too shocked at his words, at his sincerity, she never expected him to acknowledge her, albeit subtly, much less thank her. Meg dabbed her eyes, no she didn't have an emotional connection to Connor, just a bit sentimental because one of her staff members had won an honorable award.

When Connor returned to his seat, he didn't look at Meg, and she avoided conversation by sipping her water. Thankfully flocks of reporters, friends, and acquaintances swarmed around and congratulated him. Avoiding conversation with the media and fellow coaches, she clung to Marie and asked about her family. It wasn't a ploy; the Randolphs were kind. She loved hearing the pride in their voices when they talked about their daughters and grandchildren.

Nearly an hour later, on her way back from another trip to the ladies' room, Connor sneaked up behind her and whispered in her ear. "You ready to head back home?"

She flushed at the feel of his breath on her neck and nodded. They said their goodbyes to Greg and Marie and left the banquet hall. The night turned extremely brisk and Meg wished she hadn't been so hot and bothered by Connor earlier and remembered her coat. No sooner had the thought entered her mind then she felt the weight and warmth of Connor's suit coat around her shoulders.

"Thanks." She pulled the coat closer around her body and breathed in his scent. Clean. Not too musky. Warm and refreshing. The fancy Audi didn't take long to warm up—must be why they cost so much—and in minutes, the open turnpike lay ahead of them, Manchester and all its haunting memories behind.

"You've heard it a hundred times, but congratulations. I don't know much, really anything, about the other guys, but I'd say you were definitely deserving."

"Thanks."

"Are you going to tell me what the scandal was all about?"

His jaw tensed and his hands gripped the steering wheel tighter. "I'm sure you've heard rumors."

"Honestly, no. You evaded the conversation anytime anyone brought up your last nomination."

Connor sighed and relaxed his grip on the wheel. "I was nominated four years ago."

"And that's scandalous?"

"No, I shouldn't have been nominated at all. We had a losing season and I…let's just say I was a little arrogant. Shocking, I know."

"You don't have to win the state championship to be deserving of a coach's award."

"Gee, you sound like you're defending me. I wish I had this on camera."

Meg turned and smiled at him. "You're uncomfortable talking about this. I don't believe I've ever seen you embarrassed before." She liked that he had a weakness. It proved her test-tube theory wrong. Granted she had no idea what was so scandalous, but she enjoyed watching him squirm.

"It was my first year back, my first year as a high school football coach and I brought my family, some of my players, and my coaches to the banquet. I was pretty sure I was a shoe-in for the win, not that I would admit it meant much to me, a measly high school coaching award. And I may have been a bit…cocky about it. Anyway, a few guys at the banquet, including me, had a little too much to drink. They were pissed I was nominated my first year back and said it was because of my *name* and not my performance. At least not on the Newhall High field. I roughed up a few guys who were twice my age and thirty pounds lighter."

"Your *name*?" she snorted. "Sorry to break it to you, McKay, but they're right. Being a hot shot around Newhall isn't much to brag about."

He didn't say a word but eyed her questioningly, raising a disbelieving brow. "You don't know about my life before I came to NHS?"

She tensed. "I don't make it a habit of snooping in the personnel files of my staff. Is there something I should be aware of? Do you have a record?"

The boyish grin reappeared and his mood lifted which quickly calmed her nerves. "No record. Well, not that kind."

Understanding the conversation was over, she moved on. "I really liked Greg and Marie. I didn't want to be rude and ask them, but why did they move away from Newhall? It sounded like they had so many wonderful friends and memories."

"Lisa, their oldest daughter lives down here. She lost her husband a few years ago in Iraq, and she and the kids had a hard time dealing. Greg and Marie moved down here to be with the kids while Lisa works. It's been hard on all of them, but Lisa is finally moving on."

"How awful. But wonderful to have such loving and devoted parents."

Meg watched the city lights disappear as they headed north toward the country. The memories of her parents more distant with each passing year. It became more and more difficult to remember what they looked like. If she didn't have the few pictures of them, she knew their faces would be forgotten. She could still picture the news coverage of the airplane crash that killed them when she was five. Thankfully she had Gram and Gramps. While her upbringing was unconventional and old-fashioned, at least she had the love and support of her grandparents. They meant well, even if life hadn't worked out as planned.

"So is Emma's father still in the mix?"

His question caught her off guard. "No." She toyed with her bracelet as she looked out into the ebony sky.

"Sorry, didn't mean to bring up a—"

"Just forget about it, okay?"

They drove in silence for the remainder of the trip and Meg stifled a yawn as she forced herself to stay awake. But the comfort of the leather seat, the protective feeling of Connor's coat around her body and the lull of the easy listening tunes on the radio made it more and more difficult to stay awake. For the first time in…ever, she felt safe with a man.

Chapter Six

Having to face the girl you went out with after a bad date sucked.

Having her as your boss really sucked.

Kissing her and then having her freak out and stare at you like you were a monster really, *really* sucked.

Connor felt like shit, and he didn't even know why. She had looked so sweet sleeping in his car.

Her soft face turned toward him, her lips slightly open. He'd wanted to pull over and take her right then and there in the passenger seat of his car, but he didn't think his incredibly sexy boss would be impressed.

Instead, he'd pulled up to her house, turned off the car and waited for her to wake. When she didn't respond to his gentle nudges, he'd kissed her. Her supple lips were so inviting. And she kissed him back. Okay, maybe she'd been sleeping and didn't realize exactly what she was doing, but she moaned. She *moaned* and, though completely turned on, he restrained himself. When she opened her eyes she freaked. Screamed like he was some monster and ran into her house, refusing to open the door or explain her reaction. After having a one-sided conversation with her front door, he got back in his car and left. He had checked his breath a few miles before reaching her place and even popped a breath mint before waking her up. What the hell went wrong?

The woman remained a mystery. She drove him nuts and wild. She was domineering and a bit conceited, yet she had a soft, caring, even vulnerable side to her. Typically Connor went for the easy-to-read bimbo who was good for a night out and a roll in the sack. No strings. No commitments. He'd had a high-maintenance chick once and that didn't work out so well.

Mustering up as much courage—since when did he have to *muster* courage?—as he could find, he opened the door to the main office and greeted Barbara.

"Morning, beautiful. The boss in?"

"Good morning, Connor. Congratulations on your win. We knew this was your year." She stood up and hugged him and quickly sat back in her chair, a little red escaping her cheeks. "Ms. Fulton just got back from a meeting and has a parent conference in ten minutes."

"Thanks." He strolled past the secretary's desk and tapped on Meg's open door. She looked up from the file she was reading and quickly took off her glasses.

"McKay. Good morning. What can I do for you? I have a meeting in a few minutes so I really don't have time right now." She stood, all business-like, closed the file, and put it on top of her closed laptop.

Damn she was pretty. Her hair pulled up out of her face—he liked the sexy flowing hair better, but the professional look was better for his libido—and her navy suit tailored to reflect business, but also flashed woman.

"I wanted to thank you for coming along Friday night." No, he wanted to talk about the kiss that went wrong but bringing it up with Barbara's ultrasonic hearing would not go over so well.

"Sure. No problem. Just doing my job." She pulled the strap to her briefcase over her shoulder and made it clear she was leaving her office. Only Connor didn't budge. They stood facing each other in her doorway. The citrus smell of her shampoo filled the air and brought back the sensation of touching her silky hair and taste of her sweet lips.

She was nervous. He could tell by the way she kept adjusting the lapels on her jacket and tucking imaginary stray hairs behind her ears. Not wanting to frighten her, but needing to show her he meant no disrespect, he smiled. And not the boyish grin he used to work himself out of all sorts of jams, or into a woman's bed, but a sincere, honest to goodness smile.

"Okay, then. See ya around." He turned and nearly stomped out of the office and down the hallway to his classroom, wondering why this woman who hated him, flirted with him, and feared him, had such an effect on him.

"It'll be fun. Come on. You'll see us in a whole new light," Annie teased as she made herself comfortable in Meg's office chair. Her new friend, her only friend, had a lot of clout with the staff. She was head of the teacher's association, a department head and quite popular with the students as well. Everyone loved her and for some reason Meg couldn't fathom, the popular woman had befriended her.

Meg laughed. "And you think that's the line to use to get me to go out to a bar with my staff?"

"We've been going to Martha's once a month for the last…gosh, I don't know how long, at least ten, twelve years."

"I'm not really part of your crowd."

"Crowd? Honey, everyone is invited. While a large part of the Friday afternoon cliental may be teachers, it's not like we have a secret club. The whole staff knows about Friday afternoons at Martha's. Always a different mix of people there."

Meg played with the small sapphire ring on her right hand. "I guess I'll stop by for one drink."

Annie's round, pudgy cheeks widened. "Awesome! Grab your purse. You can follow me."

Not giving her much of a choice, Meg locked up her office and followed Annie to the parking lot. It pleased her that she was making friends, well a friend, and was invited into the social circle, but she also feared rejection. What if the teachers resented her being there? Who wanted to hang out with the school principal?

Friday being casual day, Meg wore navy slacks and a cream-colored cashmere sweater. The last thing she wanted was to appear standoffish. At least she wasn't wearing a suit. She drove by the bar on her way home from school and often recognized the cars in the parking lot, but socializing was never her specialty. She tried that once and had been reaping the consequences ever since.

Nervous, she got out of her practical sedan and tugged at the hem of her sweater, while Annie finished a call on her cell.

A few moments later, Annie ended the call and tossed her phone in her purse before climbing out of her car. "Our girls have formed quite the friendship. Emma's at Paige's apartment and they're getting dolled up for a double date. Even though my girl is twenty-two and lives on her own, I love how she still checks in with me. She knows her mama worries too much."

Another thing they had in common. Meg always thought she was over-protective, and hearing Annie talk about her daughter in a similar fashion eased her insecurities as a mother some. No matter how old Emma was, Meg would always worry.

Annie led the way into the bar. Inside, the walls and floors were covered in clapboard, rustic but clean. Dark tin sconces and chandeliers dimmed the lighting and made for a relaxed atmosphere while sports memorabilia lined the walls. From the Boston Red Sox to the Newhall High teams. Very local. Very New England. Very unlike Meg.

Annie walked up to the large oak bar and made introductions. She gestured to the bartender. "Mandy, this is Meg. Meg, Mandy. She makes the meanest margaritas around."

"How about a pitcher," Mandy stated rather than asked and began pouring the tequila before Annie could reply.

"Perfect."

Minutes later, pitcher in hand, Meg followed Annie to the back of the bar. Loud laughter brought her attention to the back of the restaurant where she noticed four tables of her colleagues. They all turned to welcome the new arrivals and made extra noise when they saw Meg. Welcoming noise. They were actually pleased to see her. A lump formed in her throat as she listened to everyone's sincere excitement about her being there. No one shunned her or seemed annoyed that their principal was hanging out with them. Instead they all beckoned her to sit next to them. Annie made her decision easy by pulling out two chairs and setting the pitcher and glasses on the table in front of them.

"Meg, next round's on me," shouted Bobby. He wasn't someone she expected to find here. A physics teacher. Old school. He wore polyester and had a comb-over, the classic geek. He sat with Jeanne, the trendy librarian, Claire, the field hockey coach and math teacher, and Barbara. The next table held another eclectic mix of teachers.

"Thank you, Bobby, but I'll be lucky if I make it through the first pitcher." Meg settled in her chair and made herself comfortable while Annie poured her a drink.

"Seriously, Meg, I need to know where you shop. You always look like you stepped off a runway," Claire said.

Claire, rugged and athletic as any male coach on the field, attempted to make her short, stocky build feminine during the school day.

"Actually, I'm a terrible shopper and I probably couldn't dress myself without Emma and Tracy's help. My best friend is a personal shopper in New York and sends me sample clothes all the time."

"Call me ignorant, but what the heck are *sample* clothes?" Jeanne asked.

Meg turned to her left, sipped her near empty margarita. "New clothing lines designers send out to their regular clients. They get their opinions of what works, doesn't work, and changes that need to be made. There are also other samples in random sizes, colors, and styles to the stores and then the stores pick and choose the right clothing for their cliental. Tracy obtains a ton of stuff and I reap the benefits." She shrugged and polished off her drink.

"If they have an overload of size fourteen tell your girlfriend to send it on my way," Annie chimed in as she poured Meg another glass.

Reaching for the basket of peanuts, Meg started to correct Annie when she spotted Connor at the other end of the bar. He leaned against a wall, sipping his beer and talking with another man, but his gaze focused right on her. She held the stare for merely a second and quickly turned away, but the heat from his eyes branded a flush to her face. Fleeting memories from their brief kiss and his concerned words he called out to her as she fled rang loudly in her ears. Thankfully, he couldn't see the effect his presence had on her. He made her have inappropriate thoughts of him that would surely get her fired.

Slowly, teachers finished their drinks and said their goodbyes as they headed home to their families. After two hours and three margaritas, Meg was more than ready to go home but still felt the buzz from her drinks. She and Annie decided to stay and eat dinner to try to dilute the alcohol running through their bloodstream.

On her way back from her fourth trip to the ladies' room, she stopped midway to her table. Annie had left, replaced by Connor. Meg had avoided conversation with him for the past few hours and did not want to start now.

"Where's Annie?"

"Gone." He smirked and picked up the menu the waitress brought over when Annie mentioned they'd stay for dinner.

"Is she okay?"

"Fine. Rick came by to take her out to dinner. She said she'd take a rain check on dinner."

"Oh." Uncomfortable with the intimate setting, she pulled at her sweater and fidgeted with her bracelet. "I guess I should be on my way too."

"Sit," he barked.

"Excuse me?"

"I said sit. You're not going anywhere."

"Again, excuse me? Since when did you become my keeper?"

"Since you had one too many and shouldn't be driving home. And since Annie had to leave and told me to keep you company for dinner." He picked up his menu and scanned the entrées.

Hands on her hips and fierce as the devil, Meg was not about to let the pompous ass boss her around. Ready to storm out of the bar just to piss him off, she noticed her purse on the chair next to Connor. She'd have to reach over him or ask him for it. Realizing she was stuck with his company, she scraped the chair opposite him back and plopped herself down. It was a trick Emma used when forced to sit and listen to unsolicited advice.

Moments later, Mandy came by with a smile for Meg and a flirtatious wink for Connor. "What'll it be, handsome?"

"I'd say you on a platter, but Jerry would probably key my car, so I'll settle for a burger and fries."

"And for you, sweetie?"

"I'll have the turkey wrap and a large ice water, please."

"No problem. Give me a few minutes."

Meg took in her surroundings, studying the plaques, the pictures, watching the patrons, anything to avoid eye contact with the imposing man sitting across from her. He made her nervous. Partly because of her reaction to his kiss the other night, partly because he was too smug, and knew how to push all the wrong buttons, but mainly because he was so damn attractive and made her heart race. She felt his intense gaze on her and tried to make it clear she wanted nothing to do with him.

Thankfully the food came out quickly and aided as another diversion to conversation. Mandy slid their plates on the table.

"Here ya go, kids. Give me a holler if I can get ya anything else."

"Thanks, Mandy." Connor didn't pick up his burger but continued to stare.

Suddenly self-conscious, Meg picked up her wrap and took a small bite. It never bothered her to eat in front of people before, but one could only tolerate so much.

"What? It's rude to stare!" She put her wrap down a little too roughly and the turkey and lettuce fell out of the flatbread.

"Do you know how rude it is to ignore someone you're having dinner with?"

"Do you understand how rude it is to invite yourself to dinner with someone when they don't want to be with you?"

Connor leaned forward on his elbows bringing his face closer to hers. "Do you know how rude it is to kiss someone the way you did and then slap them in the face?"

"I didn't slap you in the face!" She looked around after speaking a little too loudly. Connor obviously didn't care.

"Same thing." He picked up his burger and took an aggressive bite chewing madly while glaring at her.

Pulling her glass closer, Meg sipped her water. And sipped. And sipped until the water disappeared and the ice clinked as she set hear glass down. She needed time to think about a comeback, no longer having any desire to eat her wrap. Whatever buzz she had before was long gone.

"I was sleeping when you kissed me."

"You kissed me back," he said, picking up a French fry, scooping up a blob of ketchup and pointing it at her.

"I didn't know it was you."

"Who'd you think it was?"

"That's not what I meant."

"Meaning?"

"Never mind. I'm sorry. Okay? I was tired and when I woke up I was disoriented. I didn't mean to be rude, but I didn't mean to kiss you either. Now, can you please hand me my purse. I really need to go. This is awkward, and I don't want to have this discussion now."

"Okay, when?"

"When what?"

"When can we have this discussion?"

Meg rolled her eyes. "Wrong place, wrong time, wrong person. Okay?" Not to mention how her job could be on the line. "Let's forget about it and move on. Can I have my purse so I can pay for my meal and leave?"

"I invited myself to dinner, I pay." He tossed a few bills on the table and handed over her purse.

"Thank you." She pulled on her coat and waved goodbye to Mandy not caring if Connor followed or stayed behind to drink away the night. When she got to her car she felt his hand on her arm.

"I believe you meant to kiss me."

"What? You're crazy. Can we just drop it?" She unlocked her door, slid behind the wheel, and started her car.

He leaned over the door and stared at her again. "What if I don't want to drop it?" The threat was whispered, but it rang loud and clear in her ears as she drove home.

Chapter Seven

What if I don't want to drop it? What the heck did that mean? Was he really that angry with her for rejecting him the other night or did he mean something else? Or was he using her? Meg cleared her mind as she walked over to the stable expecting to find Emma gearing up for her Saturday lesson. Instead, she found Betsy Tucker talking to one of the horses.

"Good morning, Betsy."

The petite woman turned around and smiled. Her short, gray hair framed a full face and large blue eyes. Years of hard, physical work evident in her posture and skin, but her eyes never stopped twinkling. Four children and thirty years of marriage to George had been good to her. Over the past few months, while Emma had learned to ride and care for horses, Betsy often talked about her children and her life on the farm.

"Morning to you Meg. You just missed Emma. George brought her out to the ring to work on jumps. She's a fine rider. Come spring she'll be putting her competitors to shame."

"George has been wonderful with her. Ever since she was five years old, all she ever talked about was horses. The city didn't lend itself to many farms. The rural life was definitely one of the selling points in convincing her to move up here with me to the middle of nowhere. No offense. We do love this town."

"And we're a better town because of the two of you." Betsy kissed the white stallion on his nose and looped her arm through Meg's. "Let's go on out and check out our favorite equestrian."

The cold December air felt crisp and refreshing after such a confusing night. Their boots crunched on the frozen ground and their breath clouded the air as they walked, talked, and watched Emma ride Lady, her favorite horse, around the ring clearing the jumps.

"I don't mean to be nosey, but are you dating anyone?"

The question took Meg by surprise. "Um, no. I really haven't had the time or the opportunity to meet anyone."

"Hmm. How would you feel about a blind date?"

Not expecting that either, Meg laughed. "I'm not really blind date material."

"What in heaven's name does that mean?"

"I'm not very good at making conversation. Especially with strangers."

"You and I were strangers once, and look at us now. Once we start, we can't stop jibber-jabbering."

"Anyone can talk with you, Betsy."

"Likewise. How about you give it a try? Just one date. Dinner. I can make the arrangements."

"Who exactly do you have in mind? Not that I'm interested," she quickly added.

"My son, Mack."

"Son? You just celebrated your thirtieth wedding anniversary. And your sons are barely out of college. I'm a bit too old for either one of them."

"Oh, dear. I guess with all our talking these months I kept a bit of myself secretive. I didn't mean to. I'm used to living in a small town where everyone knows everything about everyone. I was married before George and had Annie and little Mack. Randy, my first husband, died when the kids were young. Mack had just started kindergarten. I met George some years later and we had two boys. Sometimes I forget that George isn't their father, not that I didn't love Randy. It was a long time ago." Betsy stared off into the pasture and smiled fondly at her memories.

"I guess I never thought about it. Annie is forty. You were obviously married before." Meg looked at the sweet lady beside her and couldn't refuse those pleading, loveable eyes. If her son was even a little bit like his mother or sister, maybe he would be the man she'd been waiting for. Not that she'd been waiting for anyone.

"Okay. What can you tell me about your son?"

Giddy excitement radiated off Betsy's face. "Oh, Meg, you'll love him. He'll love you. I can't believe I waited so long to even come up with it."

Meg highly doubted that Betsy, sharp-as-a-whip, head-over-heels in love with her husband and family *just* thought of it. Just like she doubted Betsy unintentionally never mentioned her son Mack. Something didn't feel quite right, but she owed the kind woman and going out on a dead end date sounded fairly harmless.

Later that afternoon over soup and salad in their tiny kitchen, Meg listened to Emma talk about Lady and how close they've become in the months of their training. It pleased Meg that her daughter had invested an interest in horseback riding, and she was thrilled Annie hooked her up with her family. The Tuckers were wonderful and owned a number of properties in the town. Even her rental house. Each month she made a check out to "Tucker Brothers." She had yet to call for any plumbing or heating problems, so she hadn't met any of the brothers, but would next week if the predicted nor'easter hit.

After she'd procrastinated by washing the windows, cleaning the bathroom and scrolling through emails, Meg thumbed through her closet of stylish clothes clueless as what to wear. She asked Betsy not to tell Annie about the date with her brother. She didn't want any more meddling, and if the date ended up being a bust, she didn't want to hurt Annie's feelings by rejecting her brother. The fewer people who knew, the less build up there would be.

Thankfully the restaurant where Betsy made reservations was out of town—she didn't want to run into anyone—and deemed one of the most elegant inns in New Hampshire. No way would she be able to sneak out of the house in date clothes and not cause any suspicion with her daughter. Delaying the inevitable long enough, she knocked on Emma's bedroom door.

"Come in."

Emma's bedroom had a young and innocent feel to it, something Meg never got to experience. The walls were painted with the standard eggshell color, but Emma added her own style with colorful bedding, a funky guitar lamp and lots of athletic equipment. A pair of skis stood in one corner while a hat rack hung on the opposite wall. Baseball caps, cowboy hats, winter hats, Emma could wear practically anything and make it look fashionable. On her nightstand stood a miniature white Christmas tree decorated with colored lights and miniature ornaments that Meg bought for her ten years ago.

"I have a dilemma. If I confide in you, I need your promise to complete discretion."

Emma closed her laptop and sat up. "I'm intrigued. Fire away."

Meg sat on the edge of the twin bed and held up her little finger. "Pinky swear."

"Oh, this has to be good! Pinky swear." They locked fingers and kissed each other's cheeks. Instead of a best friend to confide in, practice makeup on, and share secret crushes with, she had had her baby and her aging grandparents. But now, with her child grown, Meg realized what she had missed in life. She couldn't help but feel young and attractive when she hung out with her gorgeous daughter.

"I have a date. A blind date and I have no idea what to wear."

The look of disappointment confused her. "While I'm pumped you have a date, Mom, why so top secret?"

Meg sighed. She and Emma had grown to be best friends, more than a normal mother-daughter relationship. They were always completely open and honest with each other. If the tables were turned, she'd want her daughter to be comfortable enough to confide in her. "It's with Annie's brother."

"Oh?" Emma's eyes twinkled. "How is this a blind date?"

"I've never met him. His name is Mack, and I don't want Annie to know…she's so kind and friendly, but I don't want her meddling in my personal life."

"Mack, huh? Don't you think she'll find out eventually?"

"Sure." Meg fiddled with the edge of the comforter. "But by then I'll have a great cover story as to why it didn't work out."

"Always the optimist," Emma muttered.

"Will you help me find something to wear?"

"I can help with that."

Emma stood up and tugged on her mother's hand. "Let's check out the closet. Where is he taking you?"

"We're meeting at the Inn on the Mountains."

"Meeting? As in I don't get to meet him? What if he's a total dork?"

"Dork I can handle."

"Mom," she said disgustedly. "What's this place like? Casual? Fancy? Do you want to go for sexy? Conservative?" She snorted, "Never mind."

"Very funny. Betsy said it is elegant. But it's winter,

so I'm thinking dressy pants will be fine. And no, I don't want to do sexy. I don't have to be ultra-conservative like I am at school, but I don't want to send the wrong message."

"Okay, I see your point." Emma spent the next few minutes pulling out dresses, skirts, slacks, and blouses.

The bed soon became a giant heap of clothing. Meg sat in her robe biting her lip as her daughter concentrated on her task at hand.

"Got it. Go put it on." She held up a DKNY slimming, long-sleeve red dress with a small V-neck.

Meg slipped on the dress and stood in front of her daughter. The front draped into V-shaped pleats and had an elevated waist, the straight skirt stopping at her knees creating long legs, longer than she already had.

"I like the knee-high boots but since you're going elegant, wear these." Emma handed her a pair of simple sling-back black pumps with a thin two-inch heel.

"You are amazing. Tracy would be so pleased with your apprentice skills." Meg leaned over and kissed the top of Emma's head and walked toward the hallway. "I'll have my cell if you need me."

"Hey, Mom."

"Yeah?"

"If the guy's a total dud or you need an escape, just text me a quick 911, and I'll call you with some big emergency and rescue you, 'kay?"

"You're the best daughter I ever had."

"But if he's a hottie…I won't be worried if you don't make it home tonight."

"Emma!"

"Kidding. Wake me when you get home. I want all the details or the pinky swear is null and void."

Meg forced a scowl trying to hide her grin. "That's blackmail. We'll compromise. You'll hear all the gory details first thing in the morning. Lock up behind me. I have to run." She blew a kiss and left.

Cursing and tugging at his tie, Connor opened the eloquent doors to the fancy restaurant where his mother made reservations. The only reason he agreed to this blind date was because his mother asked. And she never asked him to do anything that wasn't important to her. Most likely a pity date. Someone Betsy had taken under her wing and felt sorry for.

Mack, honey, you'll fall in love with her the instant you meet. I just know it. Yeah right.

His mother may be a romantic, but he sure the hell wasn't. He fell in love at first sight years ago; look where that got him.

And why the hell did he have to drive an hour out of the way to the Inn? There were plenty of nice restaurants in North Conway, or even across the border in Maine. But he appreciated the out of the way place. He wasn't likely to run into anyone he knew.

What if the woman had hairy warts on her face? Hell, he could handle ugly.

What if she was obnoxious or annoying or a gold digger? No, his mother wouldn't hook him up with someone similar to his ex-wife. She seemed very excited for the date. Too excited.

Shrugging out of his coat, he spotted the maître de' who resembled one of those dorky guys in *The Office*. God, since when did he turn into such a desperate man that he succumbed to his mother's matchmaking?

"I have a reservation for…Mack," he sighed. He hated the nickname, but his mother made had already made the reservation…before she even asked—or rather, told—him about the blind date.

"Yes, your dinner companion is already here. Please, follow me."

The maître de' led him through small rooms tastefully decorated in a Victorian theme. Small tables covered in white damask linens, elegant candles and festive poinsettias added to the romantic ambiance of the inn. Not the kind of place he dined in. Not the vibes he wanted to send out to a woman who agreed to a blind date set up by a near seventy-year-old woman. He wasn't into hearts and flowers and didn't want his mother's new project to think otherwise. He pulled at his tie and, for the fortieth time in the past ten minutes, regretting agreeing to this dinner date.

And then he saw her. His eyes bulged, as did another part of his anatomy.

Sitting alone at a table tucked in the back corner of a dimly lit room, the flicker from the fireplace cast dancing shadows and streaks of light across her chestnut hair. She sipped her water and fidgeted with her ring while staring out the window into the black night.

Damn. His mother was right. Almost right. Maybe not love at first sight but definitely a whole hell lot of lust at first sight. And second sight. The lust thing never went away.

"Your table, sir. Enjoy your evening."

She smiled up at the maître d' and then looked at him. Her smile froze and then turned. She stood and called after the maître d's retreating back. "I think you have the wrong table!" Embarrassed at her own outburst, she bit her lip and scowled at Connor.

"You're definitely more attractive when you're fidgeting."

"You really enjoy inviting yourself to dinner, don't you? You'll have to leave, I'm meeting someone."

He pulled out her chair and pressed gently on her shoulder, inhaling the sweet, lemony scent of her hair. "Sit. You're making a scene," he whispered into her ear.

She sat. "Seriously, Connor, I'm meeting someone."

"Me too." He pulled out the chair across from her and sat, never taking his eyes off of her.

"Good. Go find her."

"I already did." *Hell, yeah, he did.*

Sighing, she rolled her eyes. "Don't you think it's rude to leave her stranded?"

"I do." His eyes roamed her face, taking in her strawberry pink lips and chocolate, almond shaped eyes. Damn, he never had a sweet tooth until Meg Fulton crashed into his world.

"Then go." She shooed him away with her hand, but he didn't budge. His knees brushed up against hers under the table and an uncontrollable shiver of awareness vibrated through his body.

"I believe I'm your date tonight."

"Hardly." She frowned. "Actually you probably know him. Mack, Betsy Tucker's son?"

"Ah, yup, I know him. Great guy. Smart, handsome, charming. Quite the catch. You'll have a wonderful time tonight."

A black-tie waiter came over and asked Meg if she'd like a drink.

"No, thank you, I'm still waiting for—"

"Actually, we'll have a bottle of Merlot." Connor named the brand; the waiter nodded and left.

"That was quite rude."

"Oh, I'm sorry. Would you have preferred white? The red dress made me think you were in the mood for a rich, dark wine."

"I'd prefer to have Mack here when I order." She crossed her arms, unknowingly revealing glorious cleavage, and looked across the dining room expecting the maître de' to bring someone else. He only got a quick glimpse, but it was enough to have him seeing hearts and roses. Damn. Maybe he was a hearts and flowers kind of guy.

"Okay," he sighed. "No more teasing. I'm Mack."

She stared at him, snorted, and looked away again.

"Connor McKay. Mack to my mom. And only her. I hate the nickname."

That got her attention. She started to speak, and by the scowl on her face, not something pleasant, when the waiter came by with their wine. He poured a sample for Connor, who tasted and approved, and then filled their two Waterford glasses with the rich burgundy liquid.

Connor picked up his glass and indicated to Meg to do the same. "To blind dates." He gently tapped her glass and sipped his wine. When he set his glass down, she still had hers midair, but finally decided to take a sip.

"*You're* Mack? Betsy is your mom? Annie is your sister?"

"Yep, yep, and yep."

"Why didn't you say something?"

"I believe I've been trying to tell you."

She set her glass down and leaned forward, again revealing soft, satin mounds of flesh. Connor pried his eyes away from the V her dress formed and moved them back up to her dark, exotic eyes.

"Why, in the three months I've known Annie and your mother, haven't they told me you were related?"

"Ask them." He shrugged.

"Why didn't you tell me Annie was your sister?"

"It never came up. Everyone knows we're related, so it's not like I go announcing it."

Picking up her wineglass, she stared deep into the merlot, sipped it and then brought her gaze back to him and laughed.

"Your mother is trying to play matchmaker."

"Hence the blind date."

"Only it really isn't. She knew I would never agree to go out with you and that's why she avoided answering so many questions."

She was talking to herself, processing his mother's scheme, but Connor still felt insulted.

"And why the hell would she think you wouldn't go out with me? What the hell is so wrong with me anyway?" He didn't mean to sound so aggravated but couldn't help himself. Her rejection hurt more than it should.

Startled, she put down her glass and apologized. "That was cruel. I'm sorry. I'm wondering why your mother assumed we'd hit it off. And why you agreed to go out with me when it's obvious we have conflicting interests, opinions, and ideas?"

"First, she didn't give me a name. I didn't realize you were my date. Second, we probably could hit it off if you weren't so hell bent on hating me."

She looked stunned and apologetic at the same time. A few months ago, he donned her the Ice Princess, but after getting to know her, while not very well, he realized it was all an act. Meg Fulton was nowhere near as bitchy as she liked to come off.

"I'm sorry, Connor. Look, you don't have to go through with this. I appreciate you driving all the way out here, but—"

"Oh, no. You're not backing out. We're here. Let's eat and make the best of our evening." He wanted to take her back to his place and rip the red dress off her smoking body and make her appreciate what kind of interests he actually had, but he didn't think it would fly over so well.

They skimmed over their menus; he ordered the rib eye while she ordered salmon. She evaded all personal conversation during their last not-quite-a-date, so he did what he thought best and talked about himself as a child. She obviously wasn't digging him as an adult, but she loved his family. He banked on the connection winning her over, or so he hoped. By the time their meals came he had her laughing over the image of eight-year-old Connor bringing his mother his idea of breakfast in bed on

Mother's Day—volcano cake and gray eggs.

"I don't know why the coffeecake exploded. I'm pretty sure I followed the directions, but I gotta admit it made one fine looking volcano."

"I'm sure it made your mother very happy. It's the thought that counts."

"Oh yeah, my little ol' matchmaker mother was wonderful about it, ate every last crumb, eggshells and all, but made me clean out the mess in the oven."

Meg swirled her wine and took a slow sip while giving Connor an intense stare over the rim of her glass. Gently setting her drink down, she picked up her fork without breaking eye contact. The evocative stare was meant to intimidate. Connor knew, he'd used it many times before, but he didn't think she had any clue how sexy it looked on her.

"So tell me why you hate the name Mack." She toyed with her chocolate mouse and licked her fork clean. It must have been the sight of her tongue that made him cave and tell her.

Slowly he leaned back, finished off the last few sips of his wine, and sighed. "My dad, Randy McKay, better known as Big Mack, was huge. Over six and a half feet tall, close to two-fifty. I was born a month early. Tiny guy. My mom and dad's friends called me Little Mack. Randy died when I was only six, but I have a few memories of him."

"I'm so sorry. You must miss him terribly. So why don't you like being called Mack? You've obviously made up for being a preemie. You're huge." She blushed and lowered her eyes. He decided to be gentlemanly and not comment on her choice of words.

"Most of my memories are of him yelling at Ma. He never physically hurt us, but he emotionally abused her. I was just a little kid, but I remember him saying mean stuff to her all the time. He picked on me too. Didn't believe

I'd measure up to much."

He didn't like talking about his father. He considered George Tucker his real father, but he actually felt comfortable with Meg and didn't mind sharing a piece of his past he kept buried.

"Ma still defends him to this day. Says he was stressed about not being able to financially support his family, different times back then. Of course, Ma finds the good in everyone."

"Even you," Meg teased.

Connor smiled, pleased that Meg would joke with him.

"But you still let your mom call you Mack."

"Yeah." He sipped his coffee and watched her eat the last forkful of dessert. "She doesn't do it often, but I don't make a big deal about it."

"Because it's all she has left of your father. And despite it all, she still loved him."

He set his coffee cup down and stared at her.

"And you love your mother a lot."

"Now aren't you the observant one." He forced a grin, but his insides clenched. The woman was amazing. Sensitive, intuitive, intelligent, sexy as hell, yet extremely insecure, and she knew how to inadvertently stir him up.

"I rent my house from Tucker Properties. I don't suppose you have a hand in that?"

Connor nodded. "Sometimes I'm up to my neck in it, but my brothers, mostly Cole, do the brunt of the work. I help out when I can."

For the next hour, they sipped coffee and Connor enlightened Meg with stories of growing up on a farm and having George Tucker as his new dad. Delivering his first foal, getting bucked from a wild mare, and Annie's tears when she first realized Wilbur did not go off to live on a pig farm but he was actually on her plate next to her eggs. He talked. She listened and asked questions, all to lure him away from prying into her life. So she wanted to remain a mystery. It would be enough for tonight, but next time, and there would be a next time, he would find out exactly what turned Meg Fulton on. Figuratively and physically.

After paying the check and helping her with her coat, he put his hand in hers—she surprisingly didn't pull away—and walked her to her car where they stood facing each other, oblivious to the cold. He loosened his tie and felt beads of sweat form around his neck and back. Hell, it was like reliving junior high all over again. He wanted to kiss her, but their last kiss ended in a catastrophe. But this time her eyes were wide open and sending off vibes brighter than a Vegas billboard that she, too, was interested in more than simple dinner conversation.

He ran his hands through his hair and laughed. "Damn, Meg, I don't want to scare you off, but hell, I want to kiss you right now."

She bit her lip, played with the cuffs of her coat, all while averting her eyes from his. Well, she didn't hit him and didn't say no, but she didn't say yes either. Not use to begging, he stepped closer, their coats buffering actual bodily contact, which was probably a good thing, or she'd really be scared.

She didn't step away.

Connor cupped her chin and tipped her head. He stared at her full, pink mouth for a long time, waiting for a response. After holding out as long as humanly possible, he lowered his mouth to hers and hovered over her lips, expecting her to pull away.

She didn't.

He kept one hand at his side, although it ached to reach for her, while his other gently stroked her neck. He watched her eyes slowly close and her head tilt up to him. Taking it as a yes, Connor lightly brushed his lips against hers. Their breath mingled in the cold air making clouds of steamy passion around them. He cupped her face with both his hands and then moved them behind her neck and into her thick hair, still keeping his lips soft on hers.

Tasting.

He restrained himself to light, simple tastes of her lips. Chocolate, wine, coffee, Meg. Perfection. She tasted amazing, but he wanted more. His head felt light and his body would have trembled if it hadn't been so conditioned.

Meg's hands stayed on his chest. Steadying herself or getting ready to push him away, he wasn't sure, but he liked the pressure of her hands on his body, jealous of his heavy coat. Someday, someday soon, he'd feel her hands on his flesh.

Not wanting to come on too hard, too fast, he reluctantly pulled his lips away from hers and softly kissed her cheeks, her eyes, her forehead, and then wrapped her in a hug. Feeling like the Grinch whose heart had suddenly grown too big for his chest, Connor abruptly pulled back. More intimacy flooded the light, feathery kiss and strong hug than if he had stripped her down naked and taken her in his backseat.

Intimacy wasn't his thing. Sex, yes. Intimacy, no.

She opened her eyes and looked down at her hands still on his chest and then stepped back. "Thank you for dinner, McKay. I actually had a nice time."

"Hey, don't throw *actually* in there," he teased, trying to lighten the mood.

She smiled shyly. "Well, I wasn't expecting to enjoy your company. But…I did."

"Would you like to enjoy my company some more?"

She gaped up at him, shocked.

He stammered, not meaning the double entendre, "I mean, would you, uh, want to go out again…with me. Like on a date."

"Oh, um…really?" She toyed with her coat again, her

sure tell sign of nerves.

What was he? Sixteen? Why did his body betray him with nerves? But she shook with nerves too. It wasn't fair how she looked adorable and he came off sounding like a total ass.

"Sure, you know, grab a burger or something." Better to shrug off the mind-blowing kiss as a casual end to a nice date.

"Yeah, okay. I'm pretty busy with the holidays coming up, so maybe after that."

She was giving *him* the brush off? Hell, if he could read the signs the woman gave off. "Sure. Whenever. Drive safe." He closed her car door and watched her drive away.

Damn, he was an idiot.

Chapter Eight

The bright red numbers glowed in the night and kept changing while she tossed and turned. Meg didn't know who she was more nervous about talking to: her daughter, Betsy, or Connor.

Emma had always been too intuitive. She would read right through Meg and know she enjoyed dinner with Connor, that she actually *liked* him. And Betsy. Sweet, dear, little ol' Betsy had manipulated her. Meg cringed and hugged her pillow tighter as she recalled venting about Connor to Betsy one day.

"The man infuriates me on purpose!" Meg yelled as she paced around the stable while Emma finished her riding lesson. The leaves had just begun to change, and the air was cool but not uncomfortably chilly.

Betsy sat on a stool and cleaned out Buster's hooves after her morning ride. "Have you ever thought maybe the man likes you and enjoys teasing you?"

Meg stopped and turned to look down at Betsy and snorted. "Are you kidding? I'm sorry, Betsy, I didn't mean to be rude, I just don't have anyone to talk to. Emma considers him God's gift to the universe, and Annie tells me he's harmless. I don't know her very well either and am not comfortable complaining about a member of my staff to another teacher."

She sat on a bale of hay and dropped her head in her hands. "I'm sorry for dumping on you. You're so easy to talk to and for some reason I feel I can confide in you."

"Of course you can, dear. I rather enjoy our talks and would never repeat a word of what we discuss. Trust me, I've heard Annie's share of venting over him."

Meg lifted her head. "Really? I mean what a relief. Not that I want him harassing any of the other teachers, but to know I'm not the only one he's had a problem with..."

"Oh, he and Annie have had their share of problems."

Meg had wanted to ask about them, but figured it would be hypocritical.

Looking back at their conversations over the past few months, she started piecing together the clues. How comfortable and *sisterly* Annie had been with Connor, the knowing glances Betsy would give her anytime she mentioned Connor. She learned he had a sister and twin brothers. One lived locally and graduated college a few years ago, the other off in grad school.

She closed her eyes and moaned, recalling how many times she *did* mention Connor. Betsy must have interpreted her constant reference to him as interest and her wheels went into motion.

And then there was Connor.

Handsome, charming, funny Connor McKay. He made her laugh, and she also felt the love he had for his family. And the kiss. Oh. My. God. The kiss. Not that she had much to compare him to, but wow. If she hadn't held on so tightly to the lapels of his coat, her knees would have given her away and dropped her to the pavement.

His soft, warm mouth had been magically skilled. The light kisses had made her heart flutter and her insides ask for more. When his tongue had touched hers, she was sure he could hear the rush of blood flowing through her body. Thankfully, the dark parking lot had hidden the effect his kisses had on her, for she was as red as the cherry that had topped her dessert.

And just like a typical man to totally and completely ruin the moment. She had the most romantic date of her life—okay, the only date of her life—and he wanted to *maybe grab a burger or something.* Not used to dining in fancy restaurants with men and letting them lick her tonsils afterward—no that's unfair, no need to make the amazing kiss sound sleazy, it was a far cry from a cheap feel—but after three hours with Connor, she felt like their relationship had changed. He wasn't the athletic enemy anymore, but a real honest to goodness nice guy. Even so, doubtful thoughts ran rampantly through her mind. What if this had been part of a ruse? What if this had been part of his elaborate plan to set her up? All men were the same, weren't they?

And the worst of it all…she was his boss. There was absolutely no way she could have a romantic relationship with Connor McKay.

Meg sat up and fluffed her pillows and leaned against the headboard. *Five o'clock.* No point in tossing and turning for another hour. She turned on her bedside lamp and took out her notepad and pen from her nightstand and started her grocery list.

Somewhere after *bread, cheese,* and *milk* she must have dozed off. The mattress gave way and Emma hopped on the bed, making herself comfortable.

"So tell me about *Mack*. How did it go? Did you have fun? It's six-thirty and you're awake so the date went down with a bust, or you tossed and turned all night dreaming about him. You promised. Spill." Emma lay on her belly, a pillow tucked under her chest, her newly painted fingers crossed under her chin.

Meg rubbed her eyes and laughed. "That's a lot of pre-dawn energy. I'm making a grocery list. What would you like me to make this week?"

"Lasagna, and don't change the subject."

She scribbled the ingredients on her notepad and asked, "Garlic bread and salad?"

"Obviously. Now spill it. Quit the delay tactics."

"Brownie sundaes or banana cream pie?"

Emma sat up, took the notepad and pen away from her mother, and glared. "Pie. Was it that bad? Or that good? You never go on dates. I've waited my whole life for you to start dating and now two in less than a month!"

Meg sighed. "Slow down, Drama Queen. It was…not what I was expecting. I had a nice conversation with…Mack, but I think we'll remain friends."

"That's it? Why the holdup with the details? There's obviously more to the story and I'm not leaving until I hear it."

"You'll be late for your lesson."

Emma glanced at the clock, "I don't have to leave for an hour. I have time."

She debated telling her daughter about Connor. Knowing Emma, she'd look too far into the situation and try to play matchmaker, just like Betsy. But if she didn't reveal *Mack*'s identity, then when she did find out, which Emma surely would, she'd be even more suspicious as to the secret.

"Mack is Connor's nickname. His mother is the only one who calls him by his childhood nickname. Betsy tried setting us up, but we're not interested in each other romantically. I respect him as a teacher, and that's all." Meg got up and walked to her bathroom and turned on the shower.

Unfortunately Emma followed her, not letting her off the hook so easily, and sat on the edge of the tub. "I knew it! You had another date with McKay. This is so destiny!"

The minty fresh toothpaste turned sour in her mouth, "No," she said around her toothbrush and mouthful of bubbles. "It's not." Meg spit, rinsed, and wiped her mouth before facing her daughter. "And what do you mean by *you knew it*?"

"Nothing. So did he kiss you?"

"You're withholding information Emma Elizabeth Fulton. Spill."

Emma appeared sheepish for a second but unable to fight her grin, she bit her lip and pulled her head into her shoulders as if to avoid the wrath of Mom. "I sort of remember hearing Mrs. Tucker refer to Mack as Connor. I didn't put the pieces together until you mentioned the blind date last night."

"Well, gee, thanks for the heads up."

"About that kiss?" Emma got up and leaned in the doorjamb not giving up on prying for details.

"We were both very uncomfortable being forced into an awkward situation. It won't happen again." Not exactly a lie, but she could evade like the best of them.

"Hey, did you know he used to play football?"

"I assumed since he is a coach."

"No, I mean in the NFL. He's a local celebrity around here. Totally loaded too, I bet."

"No, I didn't know. Now shoo. I need to take a shower." She closed the bathroom door and rubbed her hands across her face. The mysterious man, who apparently was an open book to everyone but Meg, his fame and fortune and his evasiveness when she called him on his notoriety all started to make sense. She needed to stay as far away from Connor McKay the former NFL player as she possibly could. The hot water didn't help her troubled mind and body. It only reminded her of the warmth and steam that radiated off of Connor when he held her tight during their passionate kiss.

One down, two to go. Betsy was nowhere to be found. There were plenty of horses in the large barn, but no Betsy. Emma saddled up Lady and talked to her gently as she always did pre-lesson, while Meg looked around for Miss Matchmaker. She knew why Betsy was hiding, and Meg was not about to let her off the hook.

"Morning, George," she said to Cupid's husband. "Is Betsy around?"

He cringed and nervously scuffed the toe of his boot into the dirt. He obviously knew about the mischief his wife had caused.

"She'll be out soon. Baking up a batch of her famous apple bread. Believe one of 'em belongs to you two ladies."

So bribery wasn't beneath the sweet little old lady. "Thanks, George. I think I'll go inside and see if she needs a hand."

"Go easy on her." He winked.

Meg found Betsy right where George said she'd be. The large farm style kitchen smelled like fall and family. People paid thirty dollars for an apple spice Yankee candle, while the Tucker kitchen smelled like the real deal for a fraction of the cost unless you counted the price of pride. Betsy wore a gingham-checked apron and bustled around the butcher block island, wiping up flour and then checking on the loaves of bread in the oven, looking like a genuine Betty Crocker. Meg stood in the doorway admiring her. She had a wonderful husband, four children—two of whom she knew quite well.

They appeared to be the perfect family, but from what Connor told her last night, she knew it hadn't always been easy. Randy died, which may not have been such a terrible thing, leaving Betsy a widow with two small children at a very young age. They'd had to move out of their home and into a tiny trailer while Betsy cooked and cleaned houses in the community. A battered housewife and stay-at-home mom in the eighties. When George Tucker had moved into the dilapidated Hanson farmhouse and began renovating it as well as the barn he hired Betsy to help clean, and when she'd proved herself valuable at painting, wallpapering and decorating, well, it was love at first sight. George and Betsy married a year after meeting and the rest is history.

Meg explored the kitchen, noticing the primitive stars hanging on the walls, the rooster cookie jar and teapot and the rustic pine cabinets. She learned last night that George had built them himself, and Betsy had stained them. When Connor was young, George had given him odd jobs around the house and barn to make him feel like a man while Annie had helped Betsy sew curtains and slip covers for the old furniture. All lovely memories he had shared with her last night over tender salmon, sinfully rich chocolate, and seductive kisses.

Lost in nostalgia, she didn't hear Betsy call her name.

"Oh, dear. Am I going to get the silent treatment? I can't stand it if I do. I'm sorry, Meg." Betsy dried off her hands on a kitchen towel decorated with cows and paced the kitchen. "I take it back. I'm not sorry. I think you and Connor have a liking for one another but are both too stubborn to notice it. You just needed a little nudging is all."

But instead of anger, guilt set in. "You've talked about your family for the past four months but never mentioned Connor was your son? You let me rant and rave about him when all along I've been whining about your son! I'm sorry Betsy. I didn't mean to insult your family. Had I known, I would have never—"

"Don't be ridiculous, dear." She took Meg's hands in hers and walked over to the worn kitchen table. They sat in rickety mismatched chairs that had as much charm as the little boy who once sat at them. "I'm so sorry I deceived you. I didn't do it to be cruel. I…" Betsy sighed. "Mack can be as stubborn as a mule. Don't know where he gets it from."

Meg laughed. "I came in here to give you a piece of my mind, but I find myself apologizing to you. How'd you muster up that one?"

"It's the apple bread. Does it every time."

"And George was in on it, huh? Got me to step right into the trap." She smiled at Betsy's twinkling blue eyes and saw the obvious connection to Connor. Growing serious, she said, "I do appreciate you lending your ear, and I apologize for all those insulting comments I said about your son, but you'll have to hang up your matchmaking hat. Connor and I had a pleasant evening." Sensing Betsy's interruption, she continued a bit louder. "However, we had some very uncomfortable moments."

"But it ended on a positive note?" Betsy asked hopefully.

Weighing out just how much she wanted to reveal to the mother of the man whom her loins ached for, she said, "Yes and no. We're not at war with one another, but we realized we are better off as friends."

"He said that?"

"Pretty much, yeah."

"And you feel the same?"

She felt her cheeks burn as she redirected her eyes and looked out the window. "Betsy, I recognize you mean well, but I'm his boss. A relationship between us would be highly inappropriate."

"Oh," Betsy sighed. "I never thought of that. Is it in the rulebook somewhere? What about Mark and Linda Sandown? They're married."

"Mark is head of the science department and Linda is an art teacher. There's no conflict in their relationship."

"The previous principal's daughter is a teacher at the elementary school."

Meg smiled and patted Betsy's hand. "It's not the

same. I evaluate my staff on a regular basis. It would be a biased evaluation if I started dating Connor." Meg rose and slipped on her coat. "Besides, I'm not interested in him that way. We're just friends." She hoped she convinced Betsy there was no chemistry between her and Connor.

Now if she could just convince herself.

Chapter Nine

Three weeks came and went and not a word about their date. Not that he expected her to come out and say, *Hey Connor, great time the other night. And the kiss, wow! Was it as good for you as it was for me?* He saw her five days a week at school, and again at Martha's, but she didn't make eye contact and had been enjoying herself with the teachers at her table so he let her be.

Twice he thought about calling her. Shit, who was he kidding? He thought about calling her at least twice a minute. He actually dialed her number a handful of times but never followed through with the call. He started over a dozen e-mails and imagined her reading them in her office all prim and proper in one of her suits, blushing and looking over her shoulder.

No, he'd keep their work relationship appropriate, but he had no desire to keep their relationship outside of work appropriate. *Again, not that there was a relationship.* Hell! When did he start using *that* word? He didn't want strings.

He wanted Meg. On a platter wearing nothing but…well, maybe the dress she wore to his banquet. Or the red one she wore to dinner. He could only imagine what she wore underneath. Meg didn't come across as a cotton girl. All satin and lace for her. Slowly, he imagined peeling off layer by silky layer, touching her soft skin, trailing kisses down her neck…

"Get out of the shower ladies, 'cause I gotta flush," Cole dropped his cards on the table snagging Connor out of his fantasies. Cole had recently graduated from college and was trying to find his niche in the world. Right now it entailed taking care of the family's rental properties, being a regular at Martha's and dating every single woman in the state.

"Punk ass kid, who invited him anyway?" Kent, Connor's assistant football coach, growled as Cole scooped up his winnings.

"Ah, you're a bunch of sorry old men," Cole laughed.

Their monthly poker game, held in Connor's basement—better known as the Mancave—had all the comforts of home: Extreme Fighting played on the big screen, muted so they could listen to classic rock on the Bose system, a long bar, pool and air hockey tables, and the crowded poker table. Usually the poker chips piled high in front of Connor. Not tonight though.

"I'll take the blame on this one," Rick said. "Annie made me bring him 'cause she felt sorry for the poor kid. Ugly mutt like that can't get a girl, so I told her we'd take him under our wings." Rick stood up and ruffled Cole's hair. "Anyone want a beer while I'm up?"

A unanimous "yeah" filled the air. His brother-in-law was a good guy, for a shrink. After Connor's divorce, Rick had tried to psychoanalyze him, mostly due to Annie's pressuring. Mano-to-mano, Rick was an average poker playing, beer drinking, pool shooting kind of guy.

Connor welcomed his twin brothers Mason and Cole into their man-circle when the boys hit twenty-one a few years ago. Their fourteen-year age difference kept their relationship more casual, but since the twins had grown up and started facing the real world, they found more in common.

Mason continued to be an odd duck, preferring to

study or tinker with computers rather than go out with the guys, but Connor didn't meddle. Tonight, he really didn't want much to do with anyone but couldn't come up with a good reason to cancel the monthly poker game. He normally controlled the game, but tonight the cards didn't fall in his favor. His head wasn't in the game; it was with a tall broad who seemed immune to his charm.

"Coach, you in?" Kent asked.

Apparently Rick had handed out another round of beers and another hand had been dealt. Damn, Connor needed to man-up. "Yeah, I call." He tossed his chips into the pot and took a sip of his beer before checking out his cards. A seven and a two. Yeah, tonight sucked.

"Great season J.T.'s having this year. Think he'll make it to the Super Bowl?"

"Maybe."

"You'll score us some tickets, right? I love watching the games here in your Mancave, don't get me wrong, but watching J.T. live in the Super Bowl would be kick ass," Cole grinned.

"Yeah, sure, whatever," Connor mumbled, not in the mood to ruminate about his NFL buddy or the football career that ended too quickly.

He folded on the next round and then went upstairs to let Rocky outside. He made a pit stop at the fridge and took out a beer before opening the door to the cold. Connor knew his brother-in-law had followed him, but he didn't have the energy to tell Rick he wanted a few minutes alone.

"Cold out." Rick closed the front door behind him and leaned on the porch railing next to Connor.

"Yup," Connor replied, taking another pull on his beer and watched Rocky sniff the frozen ground for the perfect spot to make his mark.

"You all right?"

"Yup."

"Okay, I don't want to pry. Just checking."

Connor didn't want to talk and never needed woman advice before, but he appreciated Rick's concern. "Annie send you?" Connor asked before Rick made it to the door.

"No, Annie isn't here tonight and can't see how out of it you are. According to her you're a big dumb idiot who doesn't know his ass from his elbow. Says you're pretty quiet at school these days. Not yourself."

"Yup. That's my loving sis."

"However, if she was here, she'd beg me to come out here and ask you what the hell has got you looking so aloof and cranky. But I couldn't care less as long as you're not taking all my money." Rick sipped his beer and moved next to Connor, staring out into the black night, both men comfortable with the silence.

Connor nodded and finished his beer. Rocky made his way up the steps and circled in front of the door, but Connor made no move to return inside. The air was silent with the exception of the tap of Rocky's claws on the frozen deck and Connor's deep swallows of beer. The cold air whipped through his thin T-shirt, but he didn't care.

"I think she's afraid of me, but truthfully, she scares the hell out of me." No need to say who, Rick had to realize it was a woman wreaking havoc with Connor's game.

"What's her story?"

"Hell, I don't even know if she likes me. She definitely doesn't trust me."

"Not your usual type. Have you done anything to betray her trust?"

"No. Seriously, I haven't."

"I believe you. You may be an ass at times, but you're always honest. Follow your heart, Connor. You have a good one. You've changed a lot since your divorce, and if this woman is worth it, show her who you really are. You've got to earn her trust. Not something you're used to working at." Rick patted him on the back and turned to go inside.

"Thanks, Doc."

That's what he'd do. Convince the woman to trust him. Yeah, sure, piece of cake. Hell, he didn't even trust himself.

Bright headlights brought Connor's attention back to the road. Where it should be. The Nor'easter dumped over a foot of snow in the past twelve hours, and he had a crap load of clean up to do. Connor plowed out his long driveway, which took nearly two hours, and then made his way through the rental properties he and his family owned. Plowing the driveways sucked. They took turns cleaning up the driveway and shoveling, and this storm Connor drew the short straw. Lucky son of a bitch.

The first snowfall of the season. Late, but a doozy. He saved the small cape on Magnolia Lane for last. Pulling into the driveway, he dropped the plow and pushed the snow down the center of the driveway. He could see Meg and Emma's cars safely nestled in the garage. While an unfamiliar Taurus parked along the side of the house didn't allow him much room to maneuver. A surge of jealousy erupted as he imaged the visitor looming in on his territory.

Not that Meg belonged to him, but he didn't like the idea of another man in her life. And he sure as hell hated the fact he actually felt territorial.

Normally he hated having to climb out of the truck and make small talk with his tenants, it dragged his day even longer, but today he was eternally grateful for the inconvenience.

It wasn't until he got out of his truck that he noticed her in the walkway. Bundled in bulky gray snow gear and tossing snow over her shoulder faster than any snow blower could spit the stuff, she looked more like a linebacker making a beeline for the quarterback than a dainty woman who normally struts around in do-me shoes.

"Damn, woman, you'll throw your back out shoveling like that. Let me." He reached around her and grabbed for the shovel but got knocked back by the force of her elbow to his chest and a swift kick to his groin. He lifted his leg up in defense as she made contact with his knee. The pain shot through his leg and instantly crippled him, but not before her left knee came in full contact with his thigh. Grabbing her, he fell to the ground, bringing her on top of his chest.

"Get your filthy hands—OhMyGod! McKay! I'm so sorry. Did I hurt you?" She pulled the buds to her iPod out of her ears and scowled.

He lay on his back looking up into the dark silhouette of an angel. Or possibly devil, his eyes blurred from the sudden impact so he couldn't quite tell, but she was beautiful. Pink cheeked, concerned and sitting right on top of his crotch.

"I don't know if I'm terrified or turned on," he groaned.

She scrambled off him and much to his disappointment, felt relief. He could feel a bruise forming on his thigh and his knee. Thankfully she kicked his good knee; although, he wasn't sure he could call it that anymore. Meg offered him a hand, and he accepted, struggling to his feet.

"I didn't realize it was you. I thought someone was trying to…"

Concern took over the pain. "What? Attack you? Here in your front yard?" The seriousness in her face and her pretty quick moves told him this sort of situation had happened before, or she had been preparing herself for an assault. She quickly smiled, which told him the topic would have to be pursued at another time.

"Just overreacting. Can take the girl out of the city, but can't take the city out of the girl."

But he knew there was something more. Between her reaction when he kissed her in the car after the football banquet and nearly killing him tonight, he knew there had to be a situation in her past she wanted to keep secret. And the cause for her constant nerves.

"Uh, huh. I came over to help you shovel and to grab the keys to the car in the driveway. Can't plow with it there."

"Oh, yeah, hang on a second." She turned and ran inside. Connor picked up the shovel and started clearing the pathway, his knee and thigh still stinging from the assault. Meg came out a moment later. "My grandparents are visiting. I'll move the car for you." Before he could respond she jogged to the car and backed it onto the street.

Connor moved sluggishly to his truck and finished plowing in less than ten minutes then drove the Taurus back into the driveway. Slowly he walked up to Meg, this time she stood facing him, so she didn't have to worry about a surprise attack, or rather *he* didn't have to worry about a surprise attack.

"Before you viciously mauled me, I was trying to tell you you're going to have a sore back tomorrow if you keep that up." He nodded toward her shovel.

"I guess it's only fair since you're going to have a bum leg," she teased.

"Yeah, I guess I should be grateful you weren't wearing any of those spiky heel things you like to wear. You're on quite the shoveling mission. If you need some extra cash, you're more than welcome to help me clean up the rest of the rentals."

A tiny elderly lady stuck her head out the front door. "Meg, sweetie, why don't you stop gabbing and ask your gentleman caller to come inside."

"Gran, he's just finishing plowing the driveway. He's leaving now."

"Not without a warm cup of cocoa. Come on in, young man." She waved to Connor and scowled at her granddaughter. "Meg, mind your manners."

"Thank you, ma'am. I'd love some cocoa." He winked at Meg and limped up the front steps. Her grandmother, barely five feet, stood by the door in her little old lady housecoat and slippers.

"You sit down here, young man, and take off those boots and coat. Earl has a fire roaring in the living room. I'll be in with your cocoa and you can tell me all about your intentions."

"Gran!" Meg stood behind him, kicked the snow off her boots, and stripped out of her snow pants. "His only intention is to plow the driveway."

No, my only intention is to strip you out of all your clothes, he thought. The little old lady walked off indifferent to what Meg said.

"Sorry, she's hard of hearing and doesn't see well. Sometimes she interprets things…that simply aren't. You don't have to stay."

"Are you kidding? She's like a little Betty White. Can't wait to find out what Earl is like. Who do you take after more?"

Meg snorted and he limped into the living room.

"Oh, wow. I really did hurt you, didn't I?"

"Please, don't pride yourself," he teased.

"You're limping. I'll get some ice." She fled into the kitchen as Betty White came out. "On second thought, I'd better stay here."

Connor smiled at Meg's nervousness and turned to the gracious hostess. "Thank you," he said before sipping the warm chocolate. He'd never been much of a chocolate person, but it reminded him of Meg. Her hair, her eyes, the way she licked it off a fork. The taste of it on her tongue.

"Sit down and tell us your name."

He sat on the sofa and cradled his mug. "I'm Connor McKay."

"McKay. Sounds familiar," a deep voice boomed from the doorway. He turned to discover a boney, six-foot giant Mr. Rogers wearing an outdated wool cardigan and checkered polyester pants. He imagined, in his day, Grandpa was one powerful man. It appeared to be where Meg got her height and coloring. Although Grandpa's hair had turned gray, it had obviously been dark in his day, just like his eyes. "The football star?"

"Oh yes," said Betty White. "He's the young man Meg is dating."

"I'm not dating him."

"Huh," said the giant. "Didn't you go to a banquet with him a while back?"

"Yes, but—"

"Oh, and Emma said he took her to a fancy dinner a few weeks ago" chimed Betty.

"Yeah, but—"

"And here he is making sure her driveway is plowed. Oh, dear me. Where are my manners? I haven't introduced myself. I'm Sally. Sally Way. Meg's grandmother."

"A pleasure to meet you Mrs. Way."

"Oh, call me Sally, please." She blushed.

Connor smiled. It was like stepping back to *Little House on the Prairie* days. He thought his mother had lived an old-fashioned life, but Meg's grandparents were lost in the fifties.

He hid his disappointment when he took his last sip of hot chocolate. Meg noticed his empty cup and took it from him.

"I went to the banquet because I am the principal and it was part of my *job.* We didn't realize we were set up to have dinner together, and he owns this place, and it's his job to plow." Meg seemed satisfied with her response, but no one listened.

"Meg, dear, why don't you ask Mr. McKay to stay for dinner," Sally whispered not so subtly.

"He has plans."

"Actually, I'm done plowing for the night and don't have any dinner plans."

"I'll go set an extra plate. Meg, dear, why don't you tell Emma dinner is ready? And while you're upstairs you might want to put on a nice dress or at least a ladylike skirt." Sally winked and then disappeared into the kitchen, most likely forgetting that she wasn't presentable herself. Meg ran upstairs, muttering under her breath, and Earl sat in the glider by the fire.

"Too bad about your knee," mumbled Earl.

Connor rubbed his right knee before realizing Earl didn't know about the attack his granddaughter gave him outside. "It gets stiff every now and then, but doesn't interfere with my life too bad."

"Had yourself a nice few seasons. Shame."

"Yeah." Connor didn't like talking about his career ending injury. Thankfully, Earl didn't ask anything more.

"Hey, Coach," Emma hollered from the bottom of the stairs. "I hear you're joining us for dinner." She looked much happier with his role as dinner guest than her mother did. Meg entered the living room, and he noticed she didn't "freshen up" while upstairs. Most likely to spite him, not her grandmother. "I'll go help Great Gran. Come on, Pops." Emma tugged on Earl's hand and led him into the other room.

"I'm sorry—" Meg said

"Look, you don't—" Connor said at the same time. "You first."

"I'm sorry about Gran." She tucked her hair behind her ear and played with the cuff of her too-large Brandeis sweatshirt. It was the first time he'd seen her in an outfit that wasn't meticulously put together. He liked the rumpled look.

"You already apologized. Unnecessarily," he sighed. "It's okay. If I really make you that uncomfortable, I'll leave." He started for the door.

"No, McKay. I don't mind. Really. It's the least I can do after tackling you."

"Gee, when you put it like that…" he laughed and kissed her forehead. The gesture surprised them both. "You're very cute when you're nervous."

"I'm not nervous!"

Connor laughed as he walked into the dining room.

The pot roast and potatoes tasted delicious. Emma's constant chatter of conversation jumping from her riding lessons to Christmas to her physical therapy patients kept dinner lively and entertaining. Meg and Earl ate quietly while Sally chimed in with random tidbits of information that never fit in with the conversation.

"Did you know Meggy won the science fair every year she entered?"

He could picture her as an adorable science geek. She helped out after school in the science and math help sessions, the two areas where the kids needed the most guidance. "Meggy graduated high school when she was sixteen. Her parents would have been so proud."

"Emma tells me you raised Meg?" He found it interesting that Meg never volunteered any information about herself during their drive to Manchester or their dinner a few weeks ago. He learned more personal information from Emma and dear old Sally.

"Yes, such a tragedy. Our Emmaline and Michael were victims of a terrible plane crash when Meggy was just five years old. Michael was on a business trip in one of those cushy private jets and asked us to watch Meg so Emmaline could go along. They were trying to have another baby and…" The table grew quiet while Sally dabbed her eyes.

"So what else do you want to do during Christmas vacation?" Meg asked Emma, a clear tactic to change the subject. But Sally didn't get the hint.

"Our Meg had Emma right after she graduated."

"From college?" he asked.

"Gran!" Meg blushed.

"Oh, heavens, no."

"Gran! This really isn't great dinner conversation," Meg interrupted as she refilled her plate with more potatoes, even though she still had a pile on her plate. Emma fidgeted in her seat as she fought a smile.

"She had me two months after graduating high school, and she was only sixteen. No one even knew she was pregnant. Not even Pops and Great Gran." That earned Emma a dirty scowl from her mother. Connor did a quick calculation. So, Meg was about his age, thirty-eight if he guessed right. Putting the pieces of information together with her reaction when she woke up and found him kissing her in his car, and then tonight's accosting, well, it explained a lot of her anxiety around him. He couldn't picture Meg as a fifteen-year-old promiscuous science geek.

Earl and Sally were still nibbling on their dinner, but Meg got up and cleared the table anyway then brought him his coat.

"Are you taking our Meggy out tonight?" Sally asked as he shrugged into his ski jacket. The phone rang and Meg rushed to answer it in the other room, which earned her a strong reprimand from her grandparents. The question caught him off guard, but he never missed a chance to seize an opportunity like this one.

"Actually, I am. Thank you for a wonderful dinner. I'll be back around eight to pick her up for our date. Tell her to dress casual. Lovely to meet you, Earl and Sally." He shook their hands and smiled as he limped through the cold air to his truck.

Two hours later, the doorbell rang. Meg opened the door and smiled sweetly at him.

"Right on time for our date. I've been anticipating this all week. Just counting down the minutes," she snarled.

He laughed at her sarcasm. "Hey, you owe me for bruising my thigh and breaking my kneecap. And by the way, if you ever tell anyone you took me out, I'll flat out deny it."

"Do you really have a bruise?"

"Wanna see?"

She blushed and closed the door behind her. "You could have asked me if I had plans tonight. You didn't have to go behind my back and have my Gran relay the message."

He helped her into the truck and waited for her to put on her seat belt. "And you would have said…?" He winked at her and closed the truck door.

When he turned down the familiar road toward the Tucker farm, she asked, "Where exactly are we going?"

"My mom's"

"Really?"

"Yeah, her neighborhood, well, the local farms, have a Christmas party every year. This year it's her turn to host. I figured we'd crash it."

"Crash it? You mean we're not invited?"

"It's my mom. I'm always invited to her house."

"Well, I can't go. Not after…well…I talked with her the morning after she set us up, and I told her I wasn't too pleased with her deceit and I made it clear that you and I are merely friends. That's it."

He pulled into the driveway, turned off the engine, got out of the truck, and hurried over to her side. Connor opened her door and helped her down, leaving his hands on her waist. "Are you sure about that?" he whispered. His lips were inches away from hers, but he didn't make contact. Meg's dark eyes closed, anticipating, and yet again fearing, the kiss that never came.

Years of self-defense training, kickboxing classes, and yoga should have built up the muscles in her legs to hold up her body, but with Connor's scent taunting her libido, her limbs went lax instead of tight. She nearly fell into his solid body waiting for his kiss, mortified when she opened her eyes and saw his twinkling baby blues darken.

Pushing him away, she strolled past him up the walkway to the Tucker farmhouse, glancing into the large bay window that overlooked the front yard. Furious that he had such power over her, she ignored him and took a calming breath.

Dancing lights from the Christmas tree in the front window reflected off the window and brought the snow outside the window alive. The laughter erupting from the house reminded Meg of another party she attended years ago but wasn't exactly invited to.

That night ended as the worst nightmare of her life. Never again would she be the same person. Over twenty years later, and she still feared rejection. She turned around to flee and bumped into Connor's hard chest.

"Forget something?" He held on to her elbows and caught her before she fell.

"I, uh…" She looked back at the house and bit her lip. "I really don't feel well, McKay. Please take me home," she whispered, tears filling her eyes.

Instead of complying with her wish, he held her close. Too close. She looked past his face at the row of cars and trucks lining the road.

"What's wrong?"

She hesitated, not wanting to make a fool of herself, still not completely trusting the man in front of her.

They'd come so far from their earlier days of bickering and not understanding each other. They'd become friends, and she didn't want to blow their friendship by having verbal diarrhea come out of her mouth, or by revealing her fears. Long ago, she misinterpreted a boy's intentions and she never wanted to do that again.

"There are a lot of people here."

"Yup, it's called a party." His eyes flickered to the window and then back to her before he let go of her arms and hunched his shoulders in defeat. "I get it," he huffed as he drew his fingers through his short, cropped hair. "You don't want to be connected with me."

He looked so hurt, and in her heart she knew it wasn't an act. Every muscle in her body told her to wrap her arms around him and tell him the truth. But she didn't. "I don't want the gossip." Not exactly the truth, but a safe alternative. "We really shouldn't be…"

"Fine. Go ahead in."

Meg stood in the driveway and furrowed her eyebrows in confusion. She hurt his feelings.

"Go on. My mom will be thrilled to see you. I'll pop in a little bit later. Trust me, no one will know we came together." He turned on his heel and stormed past his truck into the barn.

Straightening her coat and running her hands through her hair, she took two cleansing breaths, walked up to the front porch and stared at the front door. *What the heck am I doing here?* Without Connor, she had no reason to be at Betsy's party. She couldn't just waltz in and act as if she belonged. Right as she turned around to go back to the truck, the front door swung open.

"Why gracious me! What a splendid surprise! I thought I saw headlights out here a while ago. Come in, dear." Betsy smiled her welcoming smile. Dressed in a bright red silk blouse and black slacks, her short gray hair styled with a touch of hairspray, she looked so much the hostess and not a bit the farmer.

Betsy wrapped her short, strong arms around Meg and pulled her in the house. "Let me take your coat, dear."

Absentmindedly, Meg unbuttoned her black wool coat and handed it over, the entire time trying to muster up some lame excuse as to why she was standing on Betsy's front porch uninvited.

But the question never came. Instead, Betsy walked her through the house as if she were the guest of honor and introduced her to the social security collecting crowd. She didn't recognize any of the faces, but some names sounded familiar, grandparents and aunts and uncles to the students in her school. She now understood why Connor didn't regularly attend his mother's neighborhood parties. So why did he bring her?

"I don't believe you've met my boys. This is Mason." She smiled proudly at a young dark-haired, dark-eyed gorgeous man. "And this is Cole." She patted the cheek of her other son. The spitting image of his brother.

The first, Mason, smiled politely and said a brief, "Nice to meet you," before turning away, while Cole, the obviously outgoing brother, draped his arm around her shoulders and flirted with her.

"Why Ma, where you been hiding this one?" He turned to Meg and said, "I was so enchanted by your beauty that I ran into that wall over there. So I'll need your name and number for insurance purposes."

Betsy laughed and left them to mingle with her guests. For some odd reason, Meg didn't feel threatened by Connor's brother. He was younger, much younger than her and a harmless flirt.

"You're in the rental house on Magnolia?" he asked around a mouthful of mini-quiche.

"Yes, it's a very lovely home."

"You call me if you need anything. Forget about those other two lug nuts, Mason can't tell the difference between a screwdriver and a wrench, and Connor's too busy pumping iron and tossing footballs to fix a leaky faucet. I'm your go-to guy." He winked and popped another quiche.

He offered her punch and stuffed mushrooms and poked fun of Mason, his *older* brother, by three minutes, and made her laugh. She enjoyed being the center of his attention. Not that it said much, his other options had false teeth and were wearing depends, but she had appreciated his hospitality.

"Ma talks about you a lot. You and your sister, Emma."

"Daughter."

"Shh!" He put his index finger on her lips. "Don't ruin this for me. I much prefer the fantasy of you and your younger sister spending a lot of time around here—"

"Rather than her *mother*," she teased.

A cup of potent eggnog, a glass of wine and two cookies later, Connor sauntered through the front door. She didn't notice him at first. Even with her back to him, she felt his presence, the sudden storm of testosterone in the atmosphere. Meg turned when Cole stopped his story midsentence and watched the intimate showdown.

Cole grinned at his older brother, instantly picked up on the jealous, bitter glare and milked it even more. His arm went around her waist and he led her out of the living room and into the private front parlor. Unsure if the display was meant to provoke or tease, Meg went reluctantly with him.

Victorian angels and Santa figurines filled every surface of the room. She strolled to a delicate china nativity set and said, "Your mother has beautiful collectibles, doesn't she?"

"As does my brother," he mumbled.

Ignoring the statement, she studied a family photo most likely taken a decade ago. The resemblance was there, but the three boys and Annie each had their own strong features. Annie's large smiling mouth and Connor's blue eyes mirrored their mother's while the twins, whom she could not tell apart in the photograph, had their father's dark eyes and hair. The family appeared to be happy and close. It's what she always wanted to give Emma. They may not have a family photo with lots of siblings, but they were definitely happy together. A strong mother-daughter relationship was all she could give her daughter, and most of the time she felt like it was enough, but she knew Emma would have rather grown up in a large family bristling with sibling rivalry and playmates. Since she was a toddler, Emma thrived in social settings, the exact opposite as her. More like…well not like her.

"Hey old man," Cole said. She jumped and turned around, but he kept his hand around her waist. "Have you met my new lady? This is—"

"Meg. Yeah, we've met." Connor kept his death glare glued to his brother while leaning against the door jam.

"Oh, yeah, forgot she's like your boss, right?" The amusement in Cole's voice made Meg grin, she couldn't help it. Connor's jealousy of his younger brother, evident in his rigid stance, was so ridiculous she had to smile.

"Your brother has been showing me around."

"I'll bet," Connor muttered, still not removing his angry gaze from Cole's.

Cole either hadn't noticed or enjoyed taunting his brother too much to care. "Care to join us, old man? We were just about to grab another glass of Ma's eggnog."

"Oh, I don't think I can handle another glass."

"Don't worry, sweetheart. I can drive you home." Cole winked.

"I didn't drive…" she stopped herself realizing her blunder.

"Hmm. How did you get here then…*sweetheart*?" Connor mocked.

He turned his gaze to her for the first time since entering the room, and she bit her lip and glared at him. The evil eye used to work on her students, but it only amused Connor.

Cole took the hint that the fun and games were over and kissed her on the cheek. "I'm going to make myself another drink and grab a handful of shrimp. You holler for me if the beast bothers you."

Connor took up much of the space in the doorway and didn't move an inch, forcing his brother to squeeze past his massive shoulders.

Once Cole left, Connor's stance loosened. He put his hands in his pockets, as if unsure what to do with himself. Meg looked nervously around the room and toyed with her sweater.

"So what's your cover?"

"My cover?"

"You do that a lot."

"Do what a lot?"

"Repeat what I say."

She paced in front of a Queen Anne style chair then sat. "Well, half the time I don't know what you're talking about."

He followed her lead and sat in the matching chair across from her. "Uh, huh. So what did you tell my mom?"

"She didn't ask."

Connor leaned forward, his elbows resting on his knees. She didn't have time to thoroughly examine him when he picked her up from her house. Too anxious, she tossed on her coat and evaded any intrusive, embarrassing questions from her grandparents. Connor's thin navy sweater pulled tight against his wide upper body, not doing much to hide his corded muscles. Superman. He had superman's body, and she felt like Lois Lane; although, she didn't need rescuing at this very moment. Or maybe she did, and he was the only one who knew it.

At times, he mirrored Clark Kent. Nervous. Normal. Easy to talk to. And then other times he was huge. Filling the room with his muscular body, strength, and power. He may be dressed like Kent, but underneath the sweater and rear-hugging jeans—she did notice those earlier—stood a man of steel. His icy blue stare sent chills up her spine, but she didn't look away. Too mesmerized and too busy studying his features, she didn't notice the quick intake of his breath until he jumped up and grabbed her hand.

"Come on. We're outta here."

His warm, calloused hand enveloped her long, dainty fingers and she didn't let go. They rushed out the back door without anyone noticing them. The ten-minute ride passed by too quickly and quietly sans the loud thumping of her heart. Was he mad at her? She hadn't been fair to him and she knew it, but she didn't know how to make it right. Her heart and her head were telling her two different things.

The truck idled, and the silence grew thicker when he turned off the engine. Connor kept his hands on the wheel and stared out the windshield into the still night. The front porch light and the white candles in the front windows cast shadows across his chiseled face.

"I can't get a read on you." His voice was soft but didn't hide the hard edge to it.

"Sorry."

He laughed, not with humor, not with disgust, but with frustration. "I can't get a read on your 'sorry' either."

"Sorry," this time she laughed. "I'm no good at this, McKay."

"This?" He turned to her, moving his hands from the steering wheel to her hair. The gentle stroking felt so right. She closed her eyes and rested her head in his hand, savoring the touch. "Sometimes you send off these vibes, like right now, that you're…interested."

Meg opened her eyes and pulled away.

"And then two seconds later you seem repulsed by me." He got out of the truck and before he made his way to her side, she hopped down and hurried toward the house, Connor following close behind.

"I'll back off, Meg. Unless you tell me otherwise."

They stood on the front porch, he with his hands in his coat pockets, she with her arms nervously wrapped around her waist. Conflicting thoughts filled her mind. She liked the honest, caring, funny, and incredibly handsome man. But she had just as many lingering doubts. She was his boss. And he was an athlete. He had the confidence and strength that could crush her, physically and emotionally. Only she couldn't picture him using his power for anything less than honorable. All her life Meg followed the rules, sometimes at the expense of her own happiness. Never feeling in charge of her own destiny.

The time had come. She had the power. It was exactly what she needed, to be in charge of the final outcome. All she needed was a sign. Taking another cleansing breath, she tilted her head up toward the roof to the farmer's porch and smiled. The Sign.

Unwrapping her arms from her waist, she stepped closer to Connor, put her hands on his shoulders, took a deep cleansing breath, and kissed him. At first he didn't respond. His hands stayed in his pockets, his lips firmly closed, but when she moved her arms around his neck and opened her mouth to him, he kissed her back. And not tentatively.

"Meg," he murmured into her mouth.

He pulled her close and caressed her shoulders, her hair, her head. Fire roared through her veins, down her legs. Instead of turning wobbly, they burned. The image of jumping up and wrapping her legs around his waist was all too vivid. Instead she melted, her body folding into his.

Connor broke the kiss. Again. She snuggled her face

into the warmth of his neck and took comfort in his embrace. *This is nice.* He wasn't like his stereotype. He didn't set her up to be embarrassed. He didn't use her for something other than her company. And she truly believed he enjoyed being with her.

Embarrassed with her display of affection, she reluctantly pulled away, straightened her coat and ran her hand through her once perfectly tame hair.

"I guess you're telling me otherwise?" His fishhook grin nearly knocked her on her behind. God, he was beautiful.

"Looks that way."

"And what, I'm almost afraid to ask, changed your mind?"

She pointed to the mistletoe hanging over their heads. Mistletoe that was *not* hanging when she left earlier in the evening. Apparently, the matchmaking virus had made its way down Magnolia Lane as well.

"Whatever it takes," he chuckled and toyed with the ends of her hair.

"Thanks for tonight. I had fun."

"Hmm, I'm not sure if that's a compliment or an insult. You spent most of the evening with my obnoxious little brother and only a ten minute car ride with me." He stroked her cheek with his knuckles and gazed hungrily at her mouth.

"I always enjoy myself with your family, Connor. But I'd say the last ten minutes has been my highlight," she added shyly.

They kissed again, briefly, and said good-night. He whistled as he strolled back to his truck, and Meg grinned like a schoolgirl on her first date. She let herself in the house and closed the door behind her, skipping up the steps to her bedroom, thankful the rest of the house was asleep. She wanted to keep the magic to herself just a little bit longer.

Chapter Ten

Damned if he would act like a mature adult and not call her as soon as the sun hit the horizon. Connor reached for his bedside phone but quickly put it down when he noticed it was only six in the morning. He had one hell of a night tossing and turning. The woman infested his dreams, took over his body until he woke up hot, sweaty and ready to…well, ready. He woke up alone and couldn't go back asleep.

While Meg had a way of driving him crazy, he constantly went back for more. One of these days she'd cave and give into the charm that worked on every other breathing female he came in contact with. But hell, it took her long enough. And even though she caved last night and kissed him, a part of his gut told him it was only because of the mistletoe and her liquid courage.

The comment she made earlier in the night when they first arrived at his folks' place really irked him. *I don't want the gossip.* Was it because of their teacher-principal roles? The issue had never come up before, but he knew it wasn't a conflict of interest. When you live in a small community, family tended to work together. Part of him wondered if she didn't find him good enough because of his accident, but he quickly shoved the thought aside. No, she couldn't be anything like his ex-wife. That's what always pissed him off about other women. They used him for his money or NFL status, a notch in their belt. Being a teacher slowed down the action he saw in his bedroom, and it also opened his eyes to what he really wanted.

Meg.

A private lady. He could respect that. Sort of. Then it struck him. Being new in town and the head honcho at school, the last thing she needed were teachers and students talking about her dating Mr. McKay, the notorious ladies' man. Yeah, he was bad for her reputation; she was probably bad for him too. But damn if he didn't like being bad.

"Did you do something different with your hair?" Barbara stood in the office doorway, staring down at Meg.

"Hmm? What? Oh, um, no. I just…I, I, I haven't done anything different." Meg quickly closed her laptop, sat up straight, and rolled her shoulders back, attempting to appear all business-like and trying so hard to wipe the love-struck smile off her face. If Connor kept sending her cute e-mails all day, she'd never get her work done.

"You've been different this week. New boyfriend?" Barbara wasn't one to beat around the bush, and while she treated Meg with respect, she definitely crossed some personal boundaries. "I'm sorry, Meg. I shouldn't be so nosey, but you are especially cheerful these days. Maybe it's the holiday spirit." She placed a stack of mail in Meg's inbox and went back to her desk.

Biting her lip, she quickly opened up her laptop to read Connor's e-mail again.

Friday night. Dinner. My house 7:00

Bring Emma. Or come alone.

C

Okay, not the most romantic note, but it turned her to mush. And it was sweet to invite Emma along in case she felt uncomfortable. Meg glanced at her empty doorway and hit "reply."

Dinner for two sounds perfect.

After hitting "send," she quit out of her e-mail account and picked up the mail Barbara had brought in. She didn't get too far before a dark, looming figure appeared in her doorway.

"Knock, knock."

His voice brought chills up her spine. Months ago, she believed the chills came from dislike, but today that wasn't the case. "Hello, Mr. McKay. What can I do for you?" The heat in his eyes told her exactly what he wanted, and she wasn't sure how she felt about being aroused at work. Thrilled, scared, aroused, all of the above?

"Have a minute?" He stepped into her small office, overpowering it with his body and closed the door behind him. Meg stayed in her office chair and looked up at him.

"I think I can squeeze you in."

Connor wrapped his large hands around her forearms, pulled her up from her chair, tucked her into his arms, and then kissed her roughly on the lips. "If you keep talking to me like that at work, you're going to get yourself in a lot of trouble," he murmured into her lips. And as quickly as he pulled her into his arms, he set her back into her chair and tossed a piece of paper down on her desk. The door closed behind him before she could even register what had happened.

She picked up the note and read the directions to his house. Meg smiled, folded the note, and then put it into her purse as her heart raced with anticipation.

Keeping her date, much less her new glow, a secret from Emma would be excruciatingly difficult. While Emma worked with the basketball team that afternoon, Meg called Tracy.

"Hey, gorgeous. I haven't heard from you in ages!"

"Hi, Trace. How's the Christmas rush?"

"Oh, God. I have Stepford wives up the kazoo. They're all trying to cover up the five pounds they gained since Thanksgiving, yet are refusing to go up to a size two. Seriously. How's life in small town America? How's that prick you work with?"

Yikes. She didn't realize it had been so long since she talked with Tracy. "Uh, a lot better. I actually don't mind him so much anymore."

"He and his jock friends chasing around monkey skin and leaving you alone?"

"I believe it's pigskin and yeah, he's not bothering me anymore."

"So now you're down with football lingo? You okay?"

Meg skipped to her bureau and smiled back at her reflection. "Yeah, I'm okay. Great actually. I met a guy."

"Holy shmokes, girlfriend! You gotta warn me before you lay something like this on me! This is huge!"

Laughing and shaking with nerves, she sat at the edge of her bed and sighed. "Trace, it's him. Connor."

"The arrogant bastard?"

"Yeah. But the arrogant bastard is actually very sweet."

"Honey."

"I know."

"You didn't simply fall for him overnight. You're crushing on a guy. A football guy, nonetheless, and are just now telling me about it? Sorry. I won't make you feel guilty about leaving your best friend out of the loop. But you don't sound giggly and happy like a girl is supposed to. What's wrong? He's not…"

"No. At least I don't think so. It all happened so fast. And I'm beyond giggly and happy. I mean, I'm giggly and happy, but I'm also totally and completely freaked out." She told Tracy about the blind date, the Christmas party, and the tingles she experienced every time she thought about his tall, hard body and rugged facial features. "He invited me to his house tomorrow night for dinner. Just the two of us. I don't know what to expect."

"Honey. You know what he expects. Are you sure you're ready for this? By God, girl it's about time, so I hope to hell you are ready."

"What if I'm not ready? What if I panic like I did the night after his banquet? I can't be made a fool of again."

"Do you trust him?"

"I think so. Well, more than I expected. But I don't trust myself yet."

"So tell him. You're allowed to have dinner and not sex. It's not common, but it does happen."

"Gee, thanks."

"I love you, Meg. Don't go if you're not ready. But it's been over twenty years. You have to start living your life sometime."

Their conversation left Meg confused. Tracy was right. It was time for Meg to move on. But why did she have to fall for the type of guy she'd been avoiding all these years? And why did she have to be his superior? Why couldn't a computer geek, a plumber, or a grocery store clerk make her weak in the knees and froth at the mouth? Nothing in her life ever came easily. Not even a simple date.

The following evening Emma came barreling down the stairs. "I'm heading out to the movies with Paige now, 'kay Mom?" The television did nothing to calm her nerves over the past hour as she impatiently waited for her daughter to leave so she could get ready. "Don't wait up." Even though Emma was an adult and living more like a roommate than a daughter, she still treated her mother with respect and left notes stating when she would be home. A no exception rule growing up, one Emma had not grown out of, and that made Meg smile.

"Sure. Have fun. Love you, sweetie." As soon as the door closed behind Emma, she bolted up from the couch and took the stairs two at a time to her bedroom. She forgot to ask Tracy what she should wear tonight. Casual. They were staying in. Connor may be a casual guy, but she was not. Dark jeans, nice sweater, and boots. Emma picked out a similar outfit for her two weeks ago when Meg went out to dinner with Annie.

She lathered her legs and arms with lotion and lightly sprayed herself with a citrus perfume Tracy sent her for her birthday last year. A little touch-up of makeup, a quick brush through her hair and she was ready to slide into her clothes. "Underwear." Meg looked down at her white cotton briefs and shook her head. Flinging them off and tossing them into her hamper, she opened her lingerie drawer and enjoyed the silk as it caressed her body. Compliments of Tracy, of course. The matching red silk underwear and bra had yet to be worn. She had a drawer full of silky undergarments she'd only worn a handful of times. Mostly when she had an interview and needed to feel powerful. How sexy lingerie made her feel powerful was beyond her. But it did. Tracy was right. As always.

With a final glance in the mirror, Meg grabbed her keys and headed out the door. During the drive to Connor's she second-guessed her feelings a hundred times. He wasn't the type of man she envisioned falling for. Heck, she never thought she would fall in love. Not that she loved Connor McKay. Lust after? Yes. Desire in a way she didn't think possible? Oh, Lord, yes.

The directions were easy to follow, and she made it to Connor's house in less than ten minutes. The long driveway curved and led her to a massive log home decorated with big open windows overlooking the water. Meg glanced down at the directions again. This couldn't be his home. It was more like an estate. The fancy car, the huge house, the NFL player. Shoot, why couldn't he be a plain ol' teacher? He was a Prada while she was a flea market knock-off.

Meg ran her hand through her hair, smoothing any strays, popped another Tic Tac, and got out of her car. The cold air helped cool her flushed cheeks but did little to slow her heartbeat. Before she could ring the doorbell, Connor, in all his glory, opened the door. The light from the great room shone behind him and made him glow like a Greek god. Minus the toga. *Too bad.* But he did know how to fill out a pair of jeans.

"It's about time," he said as he pulled her close and kissed her quick and hard on the lips.

"I'm not late, am I?" Meg looked around for a clock and Connor laughed.

"You've probably never been late for anything in your life," he teased, leading her into a kitchen twice the size of her rental home.

"Wow. Your home is gorgeous. A woman could live in this kitchen."

"Be my guest. I know my way around the kitchen, but you look a lot better in here than me." Connor opened the wall oven and took out three large potatoes. Meg leaned against the granite counter and admired the sexy man in the kitchen.

"Can I help?"

"Sure." He gestured with his head. "You can open the wine. Glasses are to the right of the sink."

Meg walked to the tall cabinets admiring the simple lines of the modern kitchen and the complex figure who stood over the indoor grill, seasoning steaks. He caught her staring, and she watched his light blue eyes darken. Nervously, she opened the bottle of Shiraz and poured two glasses of wine. She cleared her throat and took a sip, "Mm, the food smells wonderful."

The large island separated them, but she could sense the heat coming off of his body. Or maybe it was the grill.

No, definitely, him, she thought. Their hands touched as she reached across to hand him his wine, and if the sparks firing off in her loins were any indication of what it would be like to be with this man, then she was in deep.

Real deep.

It scared Meg to death, but she knew someday she had to trust her instincts, and tonight could prove to be the night to take that fateful step forward.

Thankfully, Connor returned his attention to the steaks and made light conversation during dinner. They talked about Emma and her new love of horses, and he shared more stories of growing up on a horse farm. He didn't pry, and Meg didn't volunteer much information about her childhood.

After the dinner dishes were washed, they retreated to the living room and sat at opposite ends of the couch; Meg's legs propped in his lap as he gently rubbed her feet.

"Tell me about Emma's father. What happened in high school?" The question brought unwelcomed tension to her gut and a tremble to her hands. She attempted to pull her feet out of his lap, but he grabbed onto her ankle and held her firm. This was unchartered territory she had no plans to share with Connor. Or anyone. Only Tracy knew of her horrid past. Of the scars and emotional damage done to her that she had yet to overcome. She squirmed and fidgeted with her sweater, her hair, the pillow, to keep her hands busy, while she stayed quiet.

"Meg, I've told you all about my childhood, my family, but I know so little about your past."

"That's not true."

"Really? Then why do I feel like you're keeping some dark, secret past life from me when my life is an open book? You can trust me."

"There are parts of my life I don't want to share. They're in the past and don't have anything to do with who I am today."

"Bullshit."

His tone made her jump, and this time she pulled herself away from him. Reaching her boots on the floor, she slipped them on, zipped them up, and then stood. "I really should go now."

"No." His grasp stayed firm on her shoulders. "Don't go. I won't push. Promise. Just don't leave." He kissed her softly and all thoughts of an argument quickly dissipated. He tasted like wine and chocolate and sincerity. She hugged him tightly as he ran his hands through her hair. "Trust me, babe. Talk to me."

Those words brought her back to reality, and she stepped away from his embrace.

"You know, you have quite a few secrets from me as well."

"Come on, don't start this. I like kissing you a hell of a lot better than fighting with you."

"Tell me about your life before you started teaching."

Connor rubbed his hands over his face and sighed. "My life is an open book. I'm not keeping secrets. You could have asked anyone and they could have filled you in on whatever it is you wanted to know. Hell, ask Google or Siri or anyone. Newhall isn't exactly the place to live if you want to lead a private life."

Which concerned her. She couldn't have a private relationship with Connor without it impacting her career. "I'm not asking anyone. I'm asking you."

He walked to the fireplace and put another log on the orange flames, sat down, and then pulled Meg on to his lap. "I was drafted by the NFL my senior year in college. I married young, played pro-ball for eight years, got injured, left the league, got divorced, and then spent a few years drinking my self-pity away."

"Oh." She didn't realize he had played football professionally, or much about his marriage or divorce, until Emma broke the news a few weeks ago.

Surprisingly, the marriage bothered her more than the football career. For more than half her life, she stayed as far away from the world of football, but the Connor she knew didn't eat, sleep and talk sports; if he did, she wouldn't be here in the same house, much less the same room as him. "Why did you come back to Newhall?"

Meg lifted her head and gazed into honest eyes. He kissed her briefly and tucked her back under his chin. "I came back here after my injury. I was thirty-one and pretty damn cocky."

"You?" she teased.

"I know. Anyway, when I realized my football career and my marriage were over, I turned angry, hostile, spent too much time in bars, picking up women. I couldn't stand being around my teammates and listening to them whine about double sessions or hear them celebrate a win. I moved back home where I could be a star again and ended up turning into an ass," he interrupted before she could speak. "No comment needed from you." He kissed her head. "Thankfully my family was there to kick me in the ass. My mom suggested I help out with the high school football team and work on my teaching degree. With my major in history, all I had to do was take a few courses and next thing I knew I landed myself a job."

"So…you were married?"

"Wow, you really are out of the loop, aren't you?"

"Hey, I didn't even realize you and Annie were related until a month ago!"

"That's what I like about you. You aren't into local gossip or trying to kiss up to anyone."

"I'm a private person, Connor. You love the limelight, which may be a problem for us."

"No, that was my problem with Amy."

"Amy?"

"The ex-wife. We dated in high school, and she followed me to Texas. She waitressed while I studied and played ball. She never had a desire to go to college, just to be a part of the parties and crowds. She liked the fame and fortune. I was a football star around here in my high school days, and she liked the legacy of being with me."

Meg went rigid and wanted to pull away. *Just like Brittany.* Too many coincidences, too many similarities, but Connor continued stroking her back, oblivious to her need to escape.

"We married after I graduated, right before I started playing pro. She loved the life. Money, big house, jewelry. While I worked, she played. We basically co-existed for a few years. As soon I was injured and my fame dwindled, she moved up the food chain. Caught her in our bed with the QB from Miami."

"Ouch."

"Yeah. So the fact that you don't care about the fame and fortune is actually quite a turn on. And speaking of…" Connor gently turned her head toward his and kissed her with an urgency she hadn't felt before. He worked magic with his tongue and leaned into her body, pushing her back onto the couch. His hard body lay on top of hers as he kissed her neck, her shoulders, and his large hands touched her waist and rubbed along the sides of her breasts. It didn't take long to get lost in the allure of Connor McKay's touch.

The contrast of the soft, lush couch on her back and strength of the man on top of her made Meg dizzy with lust, but when she felt his arousal rub against her thigh, all fears of the past pushed those thoughts aside. "No!" She shoved until Connor sat up and she scrambled to climb out from under him. The fire. The dark. The music. She felt trapped. Fear of the past came rushing over her.

"Meg, it's okay."

"I can't. I'm sorry, Connor. I can't." She ran to the coat closet and shrugged both arms into her black pea coat. "I have to go."

"You're a hypocrite."

"What?" She stopped at the door but kept her back to him.

"You want me to tell you about my scandalous past because you say it interferes with *us*. But you're stalling because you don't want to come to terms with your past. It's *your* past that keeps getting in the way. Not my divorce. Not my past love of beer and women. Not my career. You're scared and I want to understand why."

"Just leave me alone. I want to go," Meg cried, reaching for the front door, her hand shaking too much to grab ahold of the knob. Connor reached out and held the door shut. Her eyes widened with fear and she started to hyperventilate.

"God, Meg, what's wrong? I'm not going to hurt you." He pulled back and put his hands up, surrendering.

She closed her eyes, wanting to hide her fear, but a stray tear trickled down her face. *Breathe in. Breathe out. Stay calm.*

"Meg. Meg! Look at me. I'm not some monster. I won't hurt you." He wrapped his arms around her resistant body and stroked her back, holding her until she was too weak to fight him. "Talk to me. Trust me."

The way he held her, touched her, talked to her. It was different from the perilous night years ago. Connor McKay would not hurt her.

"I'll never be a normal person," she murmured into his shoulder. "He ruined me. But I'll tell you what happened over twenty years ago."

Chapter Eleven

Twenty-two years ago...

High school can be rough. Especially when you're fifteen, under-developed, and in AP Chemistry surrounded by eighteen-year-olds. Meg had been too naïve to understand the joking that went on behind her back. It was her second and last year in high school. Being somewhat of a gifted child had its challenges. She wasn't *that* bright; she wasn't considered a prodigy, but she was definitely smarter than the average kid. Scoring nearly a perfect score on her SATs at fourteen and already having an acceptance letter from every elite and Ivy League school in the northeast, Meg considered herself lucky, but nothing special.

Special was Brittany Lovely. She even had a pretty last name. Head cheerleader, popular with the girls and boys, a good enough student to make honor roll, and she had boobs. Meg got her period this past summer. Hopefully the boobs would come next. That's what the books said. Brittany wore little shirts showing off her tanned, flat belly and overdeveloped chest and tight jeans that showed off her small butt and long thin legs. Meg's wardrobe mirrored the Amish. Her grandmother thought she looked older when she wore long skirts, buttoned-down blouses and glasses. But instead of blending in with the teachers, she looked like a ten-year-old in completely outdated, unstylish woman's clothes. And oh, she had no boobs.

Meg had been popular in her own right. Most of the boys didn't know her name; they called her the "whiz kid" or "Four-eyes Fulton" behind her back, but always wanted to work with her in groups. They fought over her as a lab partner and congregated around her desk at school her right before tests. She never used her knowledge to cheat. They stopped asking her to do their homework after her first month in school. But at fifteen, Meg was too naïve to realize no one cared to be her friend, that she was being used for her brains.

There were never birthday invitations for her. Not that high schoolers sent out birthday invitations, but she still sensed the rejection. Meg overheard the gossip in the halls. She heard about the parties, and who hooked up with whom. She didn't understand what hooking up meant. She assumed dating, holding hands, the occasional kiss. That's what high school kids did, right?

Meg didn't watch television or read contemporary books, just the classics. Being raised by her old-school grandparents didn't help matters either, not that she truly believed there was a "matter." Content with her life, but wishing she had a confidant, a close friend, Meg passed her time reading and studying. Her best friend in elementary school, Theresa Haskell, moved away in fifth grade, and Meg never found a replacement. And that's when her thirst for learning grew. It started out of boredom. She read. And read. And read. She asked questions, looked up the answers and never stopped wanting to learn more.

By the time she was twelve and in seventh grade, she had aced the algebra curriculum and walked across the street to the high school to take statistics and physics. She skipped eighth grade and went straight to high school, taking classes filled with sophomores and juniors; chemistry, calculus, advanced placement English and history. She could have graduated then, but she stayed an extra year to take advantage of all the advanced placement courses Central High offered.

At fifteen, her college picked out and paid for through scholarships, looking forward to her driver's test and high school graduation, Meg turned her attention to the girls and boys she spent six hours a day with. She slowly started to notice the clothes they wore, the music they listened to, and the way they talked. And then a life-altering opportunity dropped in her lap. James Spiller, the starting quarterback and captain of the football team, sauntered over to her while she stacked her books in her locker.

"Hey, Whiz Kid, got plans this weekend?" He leaned his shoulder against the lockers and crossed his arms. The letterman jacket making him appear to be tough and confident.

Meg pushed her glasses up farther on her nose and ran her hands down her khaki skirt smoothing out the invisible wrinkles, "Uh, no. Do you need a tutor for your geometry test?"

James, popular among the students and staff at Central, wasn't the sharpest tool in the shed but had athletic talent and every college in the tristate area had been scoping him out. They never shared a class together, so it surprised her when he said her name. Although he didn't actually call her by her name, and she was surprised he knew she even existed.

"Nah, Mr. T will cut me some slack. This weekend's the big championship game. He knows I'll be in no shape to take the test on Monday."

Meg nodded in agreement, to what she wasn't sure.

"Anyway, there's gonna be a kick-ass party at Turner's field after the game. You should stop by." He winked and patted her on the head as he strolled off to join his group of friends.

She stood there speechless. James Spiller, the most popular guy in school, asked her out. Sort of. She wasn't *that* naïve; she knew he was just being friendly, but she got invited to her first school party.

As expected, Central High won the state championships and the party at Turner's field turned out to be huge. Meg's grandparents would never allow her to go to a party so she told them she was meeting a study group at the library. It stayed open until ten on Fridays, and Meg spent many weekends there burning the midnight oil. Turner's field was about a half-mile past the library.

At seven o'clock, Meg's grandmother pulled up to the Manchester Library.

"I don't understand why you need to come here to study, pumpkin. Your friends can come to the house." Her grandmother said.

Meg turned in her seat and smiled. "I need to do some research for my AP Literature class. I have a twenty-page paper due in a few weeks and want to finish up some loose ends with my research."

Her grandparents couldn't afford a computer or an electric typewriter, so Meg had to type all of her reports at the library, another reason she spent so much time there.

"Okay, pumpkin. Ten o'clock. Gramps will be here."

"I'll be waiting. Bye, Gran." Meg leaned over and kissed her grandmother's soft cheek and stepped out of the station wagon.

She stood at the bottom of the library steps and waved until the red lights of the battered station wagon were no longer visible before turning and hurrying down the road to the party. Turner's field was five hundred acres owned by the Turners, who pretended to be oblivious of the high school parties that took place year after year on their property. Granted, they couldn't hear or see anything from their farmhouse, but high school students were not known for cleaning up after themselves. Beer bottles, trash, and the ashes of a bonfire littered the small trail leading to the loud party. Over the years, logs were dragged through the woods to make seating areas around the fire, and the Turners turned their heads. As long as no one got hurt or into trouble, they'd look away.

November brought chilly nights to New Hampshire. Meg shivered in her down parka and shoved her gloved hands deeper into her pockets. The smell of burning wood and the distant glow from the fire encouraged Meg to speed up. Warmth was nearby. Maybe some new friends.

It was an impressive sight. The entire student body of Central must have been in the field. Most hung around the fire while some stayed in their cars. She heard giggling in some of the cars, figuring kids wanted to escape the cold air. The fire danced and cast an orange glow among her peers. She looked around and smiled, expecting someone to greet her and welcome her to the party, but no one noticed her.

Meg moved closer to the fire to defrost her frozen legs. She took her hands out of her pockets and held them to the fire as someone reached out and put a cup in her hand. Meg turned around and gazed into James' smiling eyes.

"Hey, Whiz Kid, glad you could make it."

Meg stared at him and watched the reflection of the fire dance in his crystal blue eyes. Embarrassed by her obvious staring, she dropped her chin to her chest and toyed with the red plastic cup. "What's this?"

"Some magic punch. Help ya loosen up a bit." He winked at her and pushed the cup up to her lips.

At first the punch made her cough, but the sweetness felt good on her chilled throat. James stood next to her and stared into the fire as he talked about how he led his team to victory.

"Oh, congratulations. I heard it was a great game."

"You didn't go?" He asked surprised.

"No," she said as she finished off the punch. "I've never been to a game."

"Wow, I never met anyone who's never been to a football game." He took her empty cup. "Let me get you a refill." He took the cup and walked off.

Meg blinked and lightly shook her head. She started feeling a bit dizzy, and her eyes blurred; she couldn't see straight. She took off her glasses and wiped them with the bottom of her coat.

"Here ya go," James said when he returned, offering her the cup.

She put her glasses back on but her surroundings remained unfocused.

"Thanks, I uh, the fire is drying out my eyes. I'm going to go sit over there." She pointed to a large boulder on the edge of the woods.

"Want some company?"

"Sure." She blinked in surprise.

Normally Meg wasn't shy, but she didn't think James wanted to hear about her author study or chemistry lab she had been working on. She always had plenty to talk about—science, history, math, English—but she didn't think the football star would be interested. He enjoyed talking about himself too much.

"Do you know what college you want to attend?" she asked as she drank some more of the magic punch.

"UConn, B.U., and B.C. are all fighting over me right now. We'll see how it turns out. They've been scouting me for a few years. I'm holding out for Boston College though. We'll see." He turned to her and smiled the crooked grin he usually directed at Brittany Lovely or one of the other cheerleaders.

But this smile was for her. She saw people laughing and drinking from plastic cups. No one paid any attention to them. Something was off. James Spiller had always been the center of attention. It was normal for her to be sitting on the outskirts of the action, but not him. He put his hand on her shoulder, then the back of her neck, and then pulled her close.

Her body stiffened, her head floaty and vision blurry, and then his lips touched hers. He kissed her. Her first kiss. It wasn't what she expected, but after a few seconds, she realized she liked it.

"Let's go somewhere a little more private," he said.

Her body took over where her mind left off. The next time Meg opened her eyes, she was sitting in the back of James' Honda, and he was unbuttoning her coat.

"Uh, what are you doing?"

"Shhh, it's all right." His hands slipped under her sweater and turtleneck and onto her chest or lack thereof.

"I, uh, don't think this is a good idea." He cut her off with another kiss and with one swift move he was on top of her and his hands found their way down her pants.

"Please, stop, I don't want to do this." Meg cried. She put her hands on his chest and tried to push him off of her, but he outweighed her by fifty pounds and the magic punch turned her arms to rubber.

"Shh, you'll like it. No one has ever complained before. Just relax." He pinned both of her arms above her head with one of his hands while his other hand held her right leg down. Meg's left leg lost all feeling, trapped between James' body and the back seat of the car.

She continued to squirm and fight him, but he overpowered her and she had nowhere to go. The car tilted, her head pounded, her eyes unable to see clearly, and her mouth unable to form any more words, and then all went black.

When she woke up, her body shivered from the cold. Half-naked and alone, in the backseat of a strange car, she sat up and the world began to spin again. Dropping her head between her legs, she breathed deep. Opening her eyes, she trembled at what she saw. Her pants around her ankles, blood and some other fluid on her thighs. Frightened, she looked around but saw no one. The fire still blazed orange and yellow flames in the distance and the sounds of laughter and Pearl Jam filled the air. Meg pulled up her pants, zipped her coat, and scooted out of the car. She ran without ever looking back.

The library seemed miles away. She had no idea what time it was or if her grandmother was waiting for her. As she neared the familiar lawn of the library, she looked up to the clock adorning the tall building. Nine forty-five. Gramps would be driving around the bend in fifteen minutes. She had until then to try to piece together the night. She remembered checking the clock in the car when James turned it on.

It had been eight o'clock. It took less than ten minutes to make it to the library and less than that for the most popular boy in school to ruin her life. What had happened to the other ninety minutes? Did she fall asleep? She was still pretty light-headed, but her vision had started to clear. The magic punch. She wasn't exactly sure what was in it, but she knew it was the cause for her blackout.

Meg Fulton, fifteen, valedictorian of her class, nerd, friendless, genuine sweet girl, had her virginity and her future ripped away. Four weeks later, she discovered she was pregnant.

The tears poured out and her body shook from the force of her emotions. Connor sat silent while she shared the most devastating and private parts of her life. Only one other person knew about that night. Tracy, her closest friend, and until now, the only one who knew about the rape. When her eyes dried and her body stopped trembling, she took comfort in Connor's supporting arms.

"What did your grandparents do?"

"I didn't tell them. It would have devastated them. I wore bulky clothes and waited until about a month before my due date to tell them I was pregnant and the father was a boy from another school who moved away. They never questioned me, but supported me in every way they could."

"It all makes sense now. That night in the car. I kissed you when you were asleep. You woke up and thought I was going to rape you. Damn." Connor shook his head, obviously disgusted with himself.

"Did the football punk ever find out you were pregnant?"

"No. I never told him. No one knew I was pregnant. I always wore baggy clothes and no one really paid much attention to me anyway. By the time I gave birth in August, most kids left already for college. I stayed with Gram and Gramps and they watched Emma while I attended Brandeis. I wanted to be a scientist. Maybe work in a research lab, but as soon as I had Emma I knew I wanted to spend every possible minute with her. Being a teacher made the most sense. By the time she was ready for school I had a teaching job. But it wasn't enough. I wanted more, so I took a few classes and got another degree in administration."

"Wow. You're an amazing woman, Meg Fulton."

"Hardly. This doesn't freak you out at all?"

"Freak me out? Hell yeah I'm freaked. I can't believe all you've been through. You're *unfreakinbelievable*."

"I've uh…" Meg shyly averted her gaze and stood by the fire. "I never had much time for dating. I'm not really…experienced."

"Hell." Connor put his hands in his pockets and looked up at the ceiling. "I'm an ass for pushing you. I'm sorry."

"No. Don't be. You didn't know. I really want

to…want to…be with you, but I'm not sure if I'm ready. I'm sorry."

"Babe." He shook his head and cupped her face in his palms. "Don't apologize. Like I said, I won't push you."

"Thank you."

The kiss had more emotion than any of the other kisses. It spoke of promises, trust, and possibly love.

Chapter Twelve

The next few weeks were bliss. While Connor never would have imagined having a secret affair could be such a turn on, he definitely never imagined he could be happy having a non-existent sex life. He kicked a few field goals, but never scored the touchdown. He respected Meg too much to aim for the ultimate score. He wouldn't mind changing the status, but for the first time he was in an honest relationship. While he and Amy attended high school and college, their relationship was centered around sex and partying with friends. They didn't talk about real issues. Amy was and will always be superficial. His alimony checks remind him of that every month.

He didn't drag out the divorce and didn't fight her when she demanded half of his earnings. Whatever. She had stuck her claws into one of his teammates' back and retirement fund before he even kicked her out of the house. He hadn't been oblivious to Amy's extracurricular activities. It was easier to ignore her affairs than to deal with divorce. But he didn't expect her to drop him like a Monday morning quarterback two weeks after he blew out his knee. She had wanted fame and status, and he could no longer provide either.

The years after his divorce he enjoyed lots of sex with lots of women and never had to work too hard in gaining their interest. He attracted the Amy type. Gorgeous, simple-minded, materialistic. He didn't mind. It kept his affairs short and simple. No strings. Marriage never crossed his mind once he signed his divorce papers, but Meg made him contemplate the idea of a relationship.

"Hell," he muttered. Since when did he start contemplating marriage? Since Meg. Connor rubbed his hands over his face and started down at the pile of research papers waiting to be corrected. It was becoming harder and harder to stay focused at work. He would go the long way around the building to get to his classroom so he could stroll by the office and hopefully catch a glimpse of her. Instead of checking his mailbox once a day, he stopped by the office three or four times making idle chatter with Barbara or Jim. And Meg. The highlight of his day was standing in her doorway, catching her off guard while she was deep in thought staring at her laptop or reading a report.

She played her part well too. Making her rounds and popping into classrooms to observe teachers had been part of her job, and she did it well. A few teachers teased him about her frequent visits, assuming their feud was still existent, trying to find a flaw in his teaching. They let others believe there was tension between them. Little did everyone know it was sexual tension.

"Hey, coach, what's up?" Kent sat on the edge of Connor's desk and sipped his coffee.

"Just struggling to get through these papers," Connor replied reclining in his chair.

"You looked out of it. Come to think of it, you haven't been yourself lately. We're due for a poker game. What do ya have going on this weekend?"

He had a date with Meg. "I'll have to get back to you on that one, Kent."

"Hot date? Haven't seen you out much lately," he laughed. "That's it, isn't it? You've got yourself a girl you're keeping secret! This is great. Who is she?"

"No one."

"Come on, coach. Spill. You've never kept your girls a secret before. They're usually hanging off your arms."

He was a good guy. They'd been friends ever since Connor started teaching at Newhall. Kent loved his wife and kids and lived vicariously through Connor's social life, keeping Connor level headed, sort of.

"This one's different, Kenny. I don't want you guys scaring her away. Let's just leave it at that. Okay?"

He threw his head back and laughed. "Shit. I never thought I'd see the day! Someone's got Connor McKay by the balls." He observed the seriousness in Connor's face and simmered down. "I'll keep it quiet, Con. Don't do anything stupid."

No, he wouldn't. Or at least not intentionally.

Nearly four months had passed since Tracy visited Meg in New Hampshire. They'd never gone longer than three months without visiting with each other. It had been easier to schedule long weekend visits when she lived in Boston, but the extra two hours north in New Hampshire made a long weekend not as feasible, and being away from Connor was not an option. She was in love.

First, she'd share the news with Tracy and then figure out a way of telling Connor. She wanted to plan a romantic weekend away somewhere with no interruptions. He had friends and family everywhere in this small town. Every time she was at his house she feared someone would stop by and catch them…eating? Possibly kissing, but nothing more. True to his word, Connor remained an absolute gentleman. But his gentlemanly behavior was driving her nuts. Finally, she was ready for sex.

The sound of a car door closing quickly followed by the ring of a doorbell had Meg rushing to the front door.

She barely touched the doorknob before the door swung open and Tracy scooped her into a hug.

"Girlfriend, you look amazing! I can't wait to meet this man of yours!"

"Not on your life! Knowing you, you'd try to steal him away. Let me have a little more time with him before he meets the infamous Tracy Spencer."

"Prrrrr, so he swings both ways does he?" Tracy knew how to get attention from men and women. He looked straight and could act the part when he wanted to, but put him in the room with giggling girls or give him a few drinks and his other side spilled out. Most people imagined gay men as stout or skinny, flamboyant or wearing a sign that said, "I'm gay." Tracy was a beautiful man. Lean, sculpted, always tan, and not a golden hair out of place. He looked like a playboy, and would probably pose for a naked magazine if asked, but he was the most honest, sincere person Meg had ever met.

"I'm going to need your help this weekend, Trace."

"Oh, I think I'm going to like this. Does it involve the football player?"

"Yeah, it involves him. I need your help in planning the perfect weekend. I'm ready to sleep with him, but I don't know how to tell him."

"Honey, he'll know. Trust me, he'll know." His eyes twinkled and his perfectly straight, white teeth gleamed with pride.

She was definitely not cut out to be a sex goddess. Tracy helped her find a romantic hotel on the coast of Maine. With the room booked, now all she needed were the accessories. Shopping for lingerie at Victoria's Secret was Tracy's specialty, but Meg needed to do this alone. Tracy grudgingly stayed behind with Emma and plastered on a smile when she agreed to let him go through her closet and prospect appropriate clothing for a beautiful Redneck—as he called her now—physical therapist.

All of the negligees were adorable, sexy, and scandalous. How could she decide what to buy? Granted she had a drawer full of expensive silk and satin undergarments, but they were all picked out by another man. Tracy, but still. What she wore for Connor needed to be special. Meg had been strolling through the store, skimming her hand across the soft nightgowns forever. How would she figure out the right one? Her first instinct was to go for the high neck, lace, flannel nightgown at Sears, but that would defeat the purpose of their getaway.

Huffing out a frustrated sigh, she peeked through the last rack of lingerie when she saw it. Emerald green, pure silk, and the most beautiful, yet sexy, piece of…sexiness she'd never imagine wearing. She rushed off to the fitting room and tried it on. The thin straps showed off her long neck and strong shoulders. An alluring V-neck dipped to the middle of her small, still perky breasts, and the shimmering material kept flowing all the way to her feet. The seductively high slit in the left side showed all of her leg, thigh, and underwear. Sophisticated and sexy. Perfect. What would she do when Connor saw her in the thin silk? Faint. Definitely. But, hopefully, so would he.

Something was up. He didn't know what, but their recent conversations didn't feel right. Meg avoided him, more than the usual playing elusive. She blew him off this weekend. Granted her girlfriend Tracy had come to town, but why wouldn't she want him to meet her? Girls did that, showed off their boyfriends. She was playing coy with him lately, not giving him eye contact and being unusually quiet on their dates. Even their kisses were reserved. He'd proven more self-control in the past month than he ever thought manageable. Hell, he should be sainted with the restraint he'd held on to lately. The constant cold showers helped a little, but this backward progress didn't make him feel too confident.

He canceled the Saturday night poker game figuring he'd be with Meg, yet here he was, sitting by himself in his cold, dark house. He could have lit a fire, but it didn't have the same allure when he wasn't cozying up in front of it with Meg. He could have made some dinner, but eating alone sounded depressing. Angry with himself for acting like a girl, he decided to be a man and march over to her house and demand to spend time her. Playing the macho card never got him very far with her, but at least he'd be able to see her and meet her friend Tracy. Hell, maybe he'd catch them wearing sexy lingerie and having a pillow fight while jumping on her bed.

A man could dream.

Connor pulled a Red Sox hat over his head and yanked his coat out of the closet. The truck didn't warm up until he pulled into Meg's driveway, but the thought of kissing her made him plenty warm. Yup, he had turned into a pathetic girl. The lights were on. A girly car with New York license plates parked crookedly in the driveway. He jogged up the short walkway, anxious to see Meg's face, and rang the doorbell. A minute went by with no response so he rang again. A deep voice called from inside.

A nearly naked man, dripping wet and draped in a pink towel opened the door. He grinned at Connor. "Hi, what can I do for you?"

Connor stood speechless staring at the man who was obviously getting further with Meg than he ever had. He'd never been around her with his shirt off, and he sure as hell had never seen her half naked, only in his dreams. Anger and disgust ran through his body. He let her lead him on for months claiming to be the abused, somewhat virgin who needed to hold on to her private life, yet here she was entertaining a naked man in her house. And where was she? Probably still in the shower that he left or maybe keeping the bed warm while her naked friend answered the door.

Inner rage burned within as flashes of Amy and her boy toy of the month flashed through his head. Not again. Hell would freeze over before he let another woman walk all over him. Been there. Done that.

"Wrong house," he said and he stormed off.

The last place she wanted to be was at Martha's having a Friday after-school-drink with her colleagues; she wanted alone time with Connor. After Annie begged and pleaded with Meg, telling her she looked like she needed a strong drink and a few laughs with girlfriends, she caved. It was straining to keep up the charade that she couldn't stand Connor. He wanted their relationship to be out in the open, but she still had her reservations as to how it would impact her job. Somehow, she needed to subtly find out if having a relationship with a staff member would be grounds for dismissal.

Little did Annie know what Meg *really* needed was to be whisked away with Connor and be free of all distractions. The insecurities remained, but not as deep. At times, doubt steamrolled her mind and body, making her wonder about Connor's true intentions. *This is not high school. Connor is not James. I am not the same naïve girl I was at fifteen.*

The weeks after she spilled her deepest, darkest, soul-wrenching secrets to Connor, he treated her like a princess, gently touching but not crossing the line to intimacy. She could tell it was hard for him—literally and figuratively—yet he kept true to his word and didn't pressure her. It killed her more than him, so she thought, but Meg knew in her heart, and in the deep of her loins, that she couldn't continue with the first base routine. She wanted Connor. Bad.

Tracy's visit gave her a newfound confidence not only in herself, but in Connor as well. She even planned the perfect way to tell him about the romantic tryst she planned at an elegant resort on the coast of Maine, but she never got the opportunity to. Barbie showed up and blew her plans to hell.

Of all the women he dated, hell, all the women he knew, Meg Fulton was the last person he ever expected to lead him by his balls and twist them until he was nearly castrated. He'd been walking around with a hard-on for the past four months all because he *respected* her. Shit, he thought he even loved her. The woman knew how to put on a damn good show acting vulnerable, innocent, and even charming. But she was a witch. Leading an entire community to believe in her innocence. It was a modern day crucible in the small town of Newhall.

Revenge wasn't normally in his character, but like the Puritans of long ago, it was all he could think of to save his pride. When his ex-wife Amy strolled her tight, lithe body into Martha's, he knew immediately what play to call. The viper had always been predictable. As soon as her sugar daddy found another woman to occupy his time, she would come running back to her small hometown in search for Connor. Spotting him easily—as if she didn't know he would be there—she sashayed her Playboy bunny body over to him. Damn predictable gold-digger.

The fake sun and bleach jobs had done their number on her over the years. Everything about her was fake: the laugh, the nails, even the rack last year's Superbowl MVP bought her. He couldn't remember her natural coloring or her original personality, and he doubted she could either.

The dumb blonde and the tough jock pair never really worked for him, but when he saw Meg breeze through the door minutes after the plastic ex-wife, he thought he'd give it a try.

"Can I buy you a drink, Aim?"

She tipped back her head and raked her three-inch nails down his chest, "Why Connor, I thought you'd never ask. I'll have a dry martini with two olives."

Amy worked her way to a table of male teachers and flirted, as she typically did, while he forced a smile and held back his eye roll before ordering her drink. Meg's presence and smile lit up the bar, and he worked quickly to turn his back on her and choked down bile as he stormed over to Amy.

"Here, let's grab a private table in the corner. Tell me what's new with you lately."

She was as shocked as him, but her seductive venom smile and obvious sway of her hips told him she was game. The next hour blurred by in a haze of annoyance. Both toward Amy and Meg. The label on his beers kept him semi-entertained while Amy rambled on about idle gossip that didn't interest him and complained about her current boyfriend, her low funds, and the incredibly boring town of Newhall. "How you can stand to live in this archaic town is beyond me. You should come back to Texas. All the boys miss you."

And he was sure all the "boys" were missing her right now. She would always be their cheap entertainment. Men saw her blonde hair and big boobs and thought they struck gold. Ha! If they only knew. Connor found it hard to stay focused on her babbling while Meg was around. He caught her eye a few times and her subtle smile, and it took all the concentration he had not to smile back. He was pissed at her. She betrayed him. Pretending to be with Amy was an asshole move, and Meg probably believed he was using it to hide their relationship. He needed to act quickly and make her realize he had caught on to her act.

The anger raged inside him. At Amy for being so…stupid, and Meg for her betrayal. Connor took a long pull on his beer, draining it and banging the bottle down on the table. He shot out of his seat, pulled Amy to her feet and grabbed her, kissing her roughly. Just the way she liked it. She squirmed, shocked by the out-of-the-blue kiss, but quickly fell into it and opened her mouth to him. He didn't want to take the kiss too deep but knew he had to in order to fool Meg. Her hands made their way down to his butt, squeezing it like a stress ball, when the catcalls from the next table started. He'd had enough. If he took it any further, he'd throw up the beer he had been forcing down. Connor yanked his arms and lips from Amy, stepped back, and gave her his best smoldering stare-down.

"Let's get out of here, Babe." Knowing she'd follow, he stormed out of the bar but not before making eye contact with Meg and smirking victory. So why did he felt like a first-class shit?

Eyes red, swollen and puffy, Meg never felt worse. She'd had her share of bad days over the years. Depression, anger, self-pity, but never had she felt so betrayed. What James did to her back in high school was devastating, but she didn't remember it hurting as much as watching Connor play tonsil hockey with some bimbo. She knew James didn't have feelings for her, and somehow being raped by a drunk, teenage boy was nothing compared to being betrayed by the man she loved.

After he left the bar with Barbie, she quickly finished her drink, said her goodbyes and hurried briskly to her car before anyone witnessed the catastrophe of uncontrolled, hypo-ventilating, dam-releasing tears that were about to erupt from her. Unfortunately, Annie intercepted her at the car.

"Meg. I'm sorry. My brother is a dumb ass and his ex-wife is a slut."

"I, uh, I…don't know what you're talking about." She cleared her throat and put on her Chanel sunglasses trying to hide her tears and the surprise at the reveal of slutty Barbie.

"Honey, come here." Annie hugged her in a knowing embrace and didn't let go until she felt Meg control her shaking. "I get it, sweetie. You two have been trying to hide your feelings for each other for so long, but it's obvious how much you two care about each other."

Meg laughed. "Yeah, pretty obvious the way his tongue licked the back of his ex-wife's throat."

"I don't understand what's going on with you both. Gosh, I've sensed the two of you have been an item for a while now. The subtle glances in meetings, the way you both have been blissfully happy at the same time. I knew there was chemistry between you guys, and tonight definitely proves me right. I won't butt in where I don't belong. You would have confided in me if you wanted me to help."

"Annie—"

"No, don't apologize. I totally respect your privacy and understand why you guys wanted to keep your relationship under the radar. But know that I am here for you if you need to vent. Forget he is my brother and remember *you* are *my* friend. That shitbag has been completely disowned."

"Thank you, Annie."

"Hush. Go home, soak in the tub, drink a bottle of wine, and tomorrow when you're feeling stronger, go storm down his door, and tell his sorry ass off. If you don't, I will."

There was no point in even attempting to sleep that night. Emma stayed home and wanted to talk about her new boyfriend, but Meg needed privacy and holed herself in her room. All she did was cry. Wadded up tissues littered her floor. The bath didn't work to relax her and she didn't want to drink, so instead she curled up like a little baby and cried and cried and cried. It was nearly three in the morning before she dozed off and was awakened around eight when Emma knocked on her door and asked her if she wanted pancakes.

She'd never been one to lay in bed all day. Meg was always on the go, always multi-tasking. House cleaning, baking, doing schoolwork, exercising, always something going on in her life. It wasn't until after she skipped out on lunch that Emma came into her room and climbed under the covers with her, spooning her like a child.

"Mama." Emma hugged her tight which only made her cry even more.

Once her crying convulsions subsided, Emma spoke again.

"Mama, I've never seen you so sad. Talk to me."

"Baby girl, I love you dearly. I really do, and I appreciate you so much, but I don't want to talk about this with you."

"It's about McKay, right?"

Meg rolled over and faced her daughter. *When did my baby grow into such a beautiful, inquisitive young woman?* "So, you knew too?"

"Knew? Come on, Mom. Why do you think I've been spending so much time at Paige's place? I figured you and coach wanted to keep your love affair top secret. I took off a lot so you wouldn't have to sneak around. It's been cute watching you sing while you cook, drive, and shower. You're in love, mom, it's so obvious."

"Was, honey. Connor and I broke up, but I really don't want to go into detail."

"Yeah, I figured you'd say that. So here." Emma handed her the phone. "Call Tracy. Talk to him. You need to talk to someone." Emma kissed her mother's head and left her to her privacy.

Meg stared at the phone. Annie and Emma were

right. Blowing out a sigh, she dialed Tracy's familiar number.

"So how's the love goddess? Did the football star absolutely love his surprise?"

"Oh, Tracy." She spent the next minute trying not to cry, her tear ducts dried up, and her eyes felt like sandpaper. Meg told Tracy about the scene at Martha's and her twenty-four hour moping session in bed.

"Oh. My. God. Sweetheart, I feel so bad. This is all my fault. I thought he'd be a little jealous and would stir up the sexual pot. I totally misjudged your jock."

"Jealous about what?"

"He stopped by Sunday morning. Honey, you didn't tell me he was *jacked.* But that's beside the point. Anyway, you were in the shower, I had just gotten out of the guest bathroom, and I answered the door. In just my towel. I'm pretty sure he made some assumptions. I figured he'd play jealous, and you'd have amazing make-up sex. I didn't think he'd retaliate. I'm sorry, princess. I'll drive up right now and clear up this mess. It's all my fault."

"No. Don't bother. If he really believed I'd cheat on him…if he didn't trust me enough…why didn't he talk to me about it? Ah!" Meg got out of bed for the first time all day and paced. "He should know me better than that! Connor McKay is a spineless, shallow man, and I can't believe I fell for him. I'm so not sad anymore. I'm pissed."

"That's my girl."

"What? Don't patronize me! Don't act proud of me! I'm not some wallflower who can be taken advantage of! And stop laughing. I can hear you! It's not funny!"

"Meg, darling. I don't believe I've ever been more proud than I am at this very moment. Take a shower, get yourself cleaned up, go find Mr. Football Star and give him a piece of your mind. You're a scary lady when your path is crossed. Go now before you lose the vibe. Call me later. Hopefully much later. Hopefully you guys have make-up sex, it's the best, and if so, call me in the morning. Or whenever you climb out of bed."

"You're insane! I'm not sleeping with him. Ever! He's a pig. I hate him. I can't believe you think there is anything to even make up!"

"You go, girl."

Chapter Thirteen

Last week Connor canceled Saturday night's poker game figuring he'd be spending time with Meg, but called it back on this morning after the disgusting scene he made at Martha's last night. He didn't know what he was thinking. As soon as he and Amy got out to the parking lot she had started groping him, unbuttoning his jeans. She hadn't changed a bit. "No" meant nothing to her. When she wasn't succeeding at undressing him in the parking lot she had tried to pull his hands onto her chest, but he wanted no part of it. Too many hands had manhandled those surgically enhanced melons; besides, he lost interest in her the day he walked in on her with another man. Probably years before that.

"I call. Coach, you in?" Kent and the other guys tossed in chips, laid down cards, drank beer, smoked cigars and made mindless chatter while Connor stewed in his misery.

"Sure." He tossed in three green chips, not paying attention to what he had in his hand. *Seven and a two. Déjà vu.* An ace and two queens showed on the board, but he didn't care. He threw away his relationship with Meg; he might as well throw away his chips. The queen flopped on the river the same time the doorbell rang.

"Hell, I'm out. I'll get it." Kent tossed down his cards

and went upstairs to the front door. Connor heard Kent's friendly greeting and soon angry footsteps marching down the stairs.

The last person he expected to show up in the middle of his Texas Hold'em game was Meg, and by the look on everyone's surprised faces, including hers, he wasn't alone.

"Meg, come to give us a run for our money? You can have coach's seat. He's practically out of chips anyway," Brad, the defensive line coach, and long-time teacher said.

"You have some nerve!" She ignored Brad's hospitality and pointed her finger down at Connor's chest. He didn't like being talked down to, so he stood to take advantage of his six-three height.

"Let's take this in the other room," he said under his breath.

"You low-down, dirty, slimy, conceited, disloyal, arrogant bastard!"

"She knows you pretty well, coach," Kent teased from behind.

"Meg, not here."

She ignored him and scowled. He towered over her, but the way she scrutinized him made him feel small, inferior. "You thought Tracy…do you have any freakin' clue at all? Any common sense? You're so hypocritical and typical!"

Before she could make a fool of herself anymore, he grabbed her arm and hauled her up the stairs and out onto the front porch. Her loud, hostile breathing and thunderous stomp of her sneakers down the front steps should have signaled the warning bells, but he didn't even see it coming. Meg jerked her right arm back and sucker punched him in his jaw. Not a feminine slap, that he could handle, but a strong right hook to his face.

"What the f—"

"Oh, don't even start with me, Connor McKay. Just

be thankful I didn't put you in a headlock, kick your balls so high you'd be tasting them with your Wheaties tomorrow morning, and then run your good leg over with my car."

"You're crazy! Be thankful you're a woman or…" he stopped himself before he said something he'd regret. "And what the hell was that all about?"

"Are you kidding me? You stroll into Martha's yesterday and suck face with your ex-wife and ask me what the hell this is about? The bimbo you sang me a sob story about because she couldn't be faithful and used you for your money? What were you using her for? A sick obsession of playing with Barbies?"

"You're totally screwed up, Babe. If you want to see a hypocrite, look in the mirror." He stood toe to toe with her and couldn't help but feel the heat radiating off her body. He was sick, he knew it, but he wanted her. Bad. They had their fair share of face-offs over the months, but none were ever this passionate. When Meg was pissed her cheeks turned bright pink, her dark eyes grew large and penetrating, seductive. He imagined them doing the same in the throes of passion. She pierced him and skewered him with her chocolate daggers, and he couldn't blame her. He wanted to kill himself for going anywhere near Amy. But that was beside the point. "You told me you were afraid of intimacy, but the second I turn my back you have a parade of naked men running through your house?"

"I…*I* am no hypocrite. I don't draw conclusions, I communicate."

"Oh," he laughed. "Is that what this is?"

"Yeah. I'm communicating. I'm telling you you're a bastard."

"Okay, I'll *communicate* with you. You're a liar. And a cheater."

Meg relaxed, stepped back, the snow crunching under her sneakers, and crossed her arms under her chest. She smiled coyly at him. "Why, Connor, please tell me why you think so."

"Last weekend? Ring a bell?" He jabbed his finger into her jacket. "You told me your girlfriend Tracy was coming up to spend the weekend with you." He smiled smugly. "And you got busted."

"First, I never said my *girlfriend,* was coming up—"

"There! You can't tell the truth for a second! Is your memory so far—"

"Let me finish! I told you Tracy, my best and dearest friend was coming up. You have assumed all along Tracy was a she."

"Oh, please," he choked. "This is classic. Even Amy never came up with such a pathetic lie."

"It's like you and your family said months ago, you're all from a small town and assumed I knew you and Annie were brother and sister. Assumed I knew Betsy was your mom. Assumed I knew you had a professional football career. We all make assumptions. I never realized I hadn't mentioned Tracy's gender. I guess it never came up. Do you say, 'Hey, meet my friend Kent. He's a guy.' I never thought about it, and it shouldn't be a big deal."

"Of course it's a big deal. You're spending the weekend with a guy in your house. You've spent the past fifteen, sixteen years with this guy, and you're telling me he's never tried to get you into bed? What is he—" The light bulb flashed so brightly over his head he had to shut his eyes.

"Wow. You're a quick one, coach. Yeah, Tracy is gay. Does that make you feel better? Your ego in check now? You've proven over and over again how much of a man you are. Thank God I found out before it was too late." She turned and stomped to her car and muttered quietly, but he easily understood. *Go to hell.*

She needn't worry. He was already there.

Signs of spring popped up along the roadside. Melting snow banks made large puddles and streams down the road. Potholes so large, cars looked like balls in a pinball machine, dodging them left and right and practically driving into the slushy roadside to avoid a bottomless gouge that could easily rip out a muffler or blow a tire. It didn't make for excellent running either. Emma figured she ran an extra half-mile today by zigzagging across the road.

The fresh air felt good on her skin and in her lungs. Listening to Maroon 5 in her iPod, she slowed down as she neared the last curve before her house. She didn't want her run to end. It felt good to get out of her house, escape the sadness that haloed her mother.

When they first started dating, before they admitted it was dating, she envisioned the handsome Connor McKay as her mom's husband. As her new dad. She'd never met her dad; her mother wouldn't talk about him. She never missed having a dad before, but ever since the image had been planted in her mind—her mom, a dad, and her sitting down to a family meal—well, she wanted it more than ever. But mostly, she wanted her mom back. She was so sad lately it broke Emma's heart.

The house felt empty now. When Connor came into the picture, he added an air of hopefulness, love, and anticipation into her mom's life. She'd never witnessed the love between her mom and the coach; they kept their dating quiet and behind closed doors, but it was impossible not to feel the excitement in her mom's voice and pick up on the perky moods. Until last week.

Angry, sure. Depressed, sometimes. Happy, occasionally. But sad, never. Emma had never known her mother to look so hurt, and she was furious at Connor for turning her strong, powerful mother into a zombie. She wouldn't confide in Emma after she returned from coach's house, but Emma knew the lashing must have been intense. She'd been on the other end of her mother's temper many times before, and it was a scary place to be. Her mother was not a person people messed with, and when she had returned from Connor's house she quietly dropped her keys into the dish by the front door and crawled back in bed.

This morning was the same as the day before. No family breakfast. Emma could fend for herself, but she liked making breakfast with her mom on the weekends. It was their tradition. Cereal, bagels, and frozen waffles on work days, but on weekends, breakfast was always a feast. This morning, she poured herself a bowl of Shredded Wheat and listened for sounds of movement upstairs. All was quiet.

Around noon, Emma knocked on her mother's door and reminded her of the self-defense class she taught at the Y. Her mother reluctantly got out of bed, dressed, and went to her class. The house was too quiet and lonely, so Emma went for a run and brainstormed ways to help her mother.

The first idea that popped into her head was to slash McKay's tires. Maybe key his fancy car, but the thrill would only last a minute and her politically correct mother probably wouldn't appreciate her good intentions. Egging his house popped in her head as a possibility, but again her mother wouldn't approve. She needed to come up with a game plan. Checking her pulse and slowing down as she neared her driveway, she looked up and recognized the familiar truck.

Connor sat on the front steps resting his head on his knees, his Red Sox hat shielding his facial expression. He didn't hear her approach until she was a few yards away from him.

"Hey, Emma. I was…uh, hoping your mom would be

home soon."

He looked pathetic. He hadn't shaved, his jeans and sweatshirt appeared to be slept in, and his eyes lacked the mischievous smile that invaded so many teenagers' dreams at night. She took the iPod buds out of her ears.

"She's at the Y. Teaching a self-defense class. She's pretty good. Could probably knock you on your ass." Emma folded her arms across her chest and stood strong as her mother's protector.

"Yeah, I know. She already has. Look uh, do you know when she'll be back?"

He stood and shifted from foot to foot making it clear he didn't want to be standing outside talking with her, but she didn't care about his comfort level. This was her mother he hurt.

"I should probably stay out of this—"

"Yes, you should," he growled.

"I won't sit by and watch you rip my mother's heart out and shove it down the garbage disposal." Okay, not so elegantly put, but she wouldn't stop there. "I don't know exactly what happened between you and my mom, but whatever you did, you need to fix it. A few weeks ago my mother was full of life, happy, singing, *singing* throughout the house. My mother doesn't sing. I know it's because of you. Then something happened, and it's probably your fault. My mom is the nicest, kindest person in the world, and she would never hurt anyone. So you either fix it or leave her alone."

"Like mother, like daughter," he mumbled.

"So, coach, before I go any further I want you to tell me your intentions."

The grin left as quickly as it came. "You sound like your great grandmother. I want to talk with your mom. Then we'll figure out if our relationship can be fixed or should be left alone. When will she be back?"

Emma puffed out her cheeks. "Here's the deal. Give

her some time to get back on her feet, and then I'll let you talk with her. She doesn't want to talk to anybody right now, much less you. No offense. Well, actually, you should take offense since you're the one who…" the look in his eyes told her she had crossed the line. "Okay, never mind. Just give her some time, okay? She's pretty shaken up right now."

Connor pulled down on the brim of his hat and sighed. "Okay, kid. I'll back off, but not for too long." He walked toward his truck but turned around before he got in. "Does she like flowers?"

"Lilies. She likes lilies." Emma unlocked the front door and gently closed it behind her. She hoped she did the right thing. Connor appeared so beat up, so terrible. Which made her smile.

Chapter Fourteen

Someone let out a long whistle. “Oh my, I’ll sign for those.” She heard Barbara gladly exclaim out in the main office. Moments later her petite frame entered, hidden behind an elaborate bouquet of flowers. Lilies. Meg actually smiled, her first in over a week. “Someone must love you a lot.”

“Oh, gosh. These are for me? They must be from Tracy.” Meg thanked Barbara, smelled the fragrant flowers, and picked up the small card hidden in the middle of the arrangement. It was just like Tracy to make such an elaborate gesture, but flowers were so unlike him. She carefully opened the envelope and slid out the card.

Forgive me.

She turned the card over, but the back side was blank. Odd. Tracy wasn’t a man of few words, and she had already told him she wasn’t mad at him. Still, it heartened her that he could be so thoughtful. Not one to make personal calls during work hours, she waited until the end of the school day to call and to thank him.

“Sweetie, how I’d love to take credit for flowers—actually I wouldn’t. They’re not very practical. They wilt and turn brown and ugly in a week while a pair of Jimmy Choos or a nice Kate Spade bag can last a lifetime.”

So the flowers weren’t from him. Which left one

other possibility, but she couldn't imagine Connor sending her flowers with the way she left him. Unless he felt guilty. Guilty about cheating on her and flashing his affair in her face. Good. She hoped the guilt ate him from the insides out, destroying that perfect body, killer smile, and talented hands.

Tuesday evening, a gorgeous bouquet of colorful tulips were delivered to her house with a card that read *I miss you.* On Wednesday, yellow roses appeared on her office desk. The message *I'm an idiot* accompanied them. Thursday's fresh daisy delivery interrupted her dinner, and her belly felt a light flutter of butterflies when she read *I need you.* The flowers had to stop; although, if she was honest with herself she would have to admit that each delivery brought a new feeling of rejuvenation, of hope, of despair. She couldn't go on giving Connor the silent treatment forever.

Feeling confident in her slimming, yet intimidating, pinstripe pencil skirt suit and sling-back heels, Meg marched into Connor's classroom after the dismissal bell rang signaling the end of the school day and the start of the weekend, kept herself poised and her expression one a poker opponent wouldn't be able to read and said, "I'll be home around five o'clock. If you want to talk." And then she marched briskly away before any further conversation could take place.

The hair, the clothes, the shoes, heck, even her scent were all supposed to exude confidence, one of the splendid tricks Tracy taught her years ago, and disguise all signs of insecurity. Even her undergarments screamed *powerful woman!* No one knew she had lacy, satin bras and panties on, and that was the point. Feeling them against her skin was like indulging in decadent chocolate and no one finding out.

Nervously pacing the kitchen for almost an hour, Meg finally decided to take off her high power duds. He wasn't coming. *Screw it.* She changed into comfortable yoga pants and an oversized Brandeis sweatshirt; she finger combed her hair into a messy bun and tackled the kitchen floor. Nothing like getting out your frustration by picking at petrified food, spilled juice, and tracked in mud.

The floor wasn't a biohazard, but when a woman got stood up by an ex-boyfriend, a cheating ex-boyfriend for whom she had taken great care to look her best, there was no stopping her cleaning rampage. Being on her hands and knees, the tiny specks of dirt magnified into the germ-catching, disease-infested grime that they were. All her focus and intensity focused on a stubborn stain on the tile floor, most likely left from the previous tenants and had no hope of being removed. She didn't hear the doorbell ring. Or the door open. Or the footsteps that led to her sweaty, dingy face that hung inches from the floor.

The dark gray L.L. Bean boots could have belonged to anyone, but only one person's presence could turn up the heat in Meg's internal thermostat this way. She wiped the back of her hand across her sweaty forehead and glared up at the intruder.

"Ever hear of knocking?"

"Ever hear of answering your door? Here," Connor held out his hand. She refused his help. Her knees and back ached, but she didn't dare show any sign of weakness as she stood.

Turning on the kitchen sink, she waited for the water to warm up and slowly washed her hands while glancing at the reflection in the window for a sneak peek at Connor. She wasn't in the mood for a fight. She said her piece last week, and he apologized through flowers. Cowardly, but nice. If he wanted to grovel, she'd let him and then politely show him the door.

Working with him every day had been difficult enough, so she might as well bury the hatchet and move on. Drying her hands on a towel, Meg slowly turned around and leaned against the counter, waiting for Connor to speak. He didn't. He stood menacingly in her kitchen, overpowering it with his body, and stared at her. His facial expression was impossible to read. Not angry, not ashamed, not happy, not anything. Her poker face mirrored his. It turned into a stare down, and she had to bite her cheek to refrain from speaking first.

Connor dragged his hands across his face and sighed. "I don't know where to start." He tilted his head like a guilty puppy, probably expecting her to help with the dialogue, but she didn't so much as breathe. "I'm sorry," he shook his head. "No, that sounds lame. But I am. Really." He paced the small space of the kitchen trying to keep a rein on his impatience and then took three giant steps and invaded her personal space.

"Meg." He took her limp hands in his. "This all looks bad, but it really isn't. When I came here a few weeks ago expecting to find you and your girlfriend having a pillow fight and saw a naked man instead I…well, I got jealous. And pissed. The pissed part I could relate to, but the jealous part was new to me and that really pissed me off."

His baby blues drooped and softened. "When I caught Amy cheating—"

"I'm not Amy," Meg quickly interrupted, stepping away from his hypnotic eyes and walking to the front door. Connor put his hand on hers and pulled her away from the door before she could open it.

"No, thank God, you're not Amy. But when I believed you cheated on me it felt the same. Hell, no…shit. It didn't feel the same. With her, I didn't really care. It was a way out. I walked in on her and then packed my bags and left. I didn't care about her but hated being made a fool of. I didn't confront you because I was scared. I didn't want to accept that you would betray me, and I was afraid I would care."

He led them to the couch and she willingly, weak

from his touch, sat next to him. "I stewed for a few days, not knowing what to say to you. When Amy walked through the door of Martha's the idea sort of smacked me in the head. I figured I'd get back at you by cozying up with Amy."

"That's nice, Connor. I'm glad you can admit you're an ass, but it doesn't change the situation," she huffed. The image of Amy in his arms, their naked bodies mingled together nearly made her gag.

"Let me finish. The entire time I was talking with Amy, pretending to be turned on by her, I thought I was going to puke. I kept noticing you out of the corner of my eye laughing, smiling with our friends. I wanted to be with you. Touch you, listen to you, talk with you, kiss you, but I was so bent on payback."

"Again, Connor. Thanks for the story, but I was there. Reliving it isn't making it any easier."

"Meg, honey, it's not what you think. I jumped to conclusions about you and Tracy, don't do the same with Amy. Nothing happened." Meg opened her mouth to argue, and he quickly finished his sentence. "Besides, the disgusting kiss to make you jealous. We left and I told her to hit the high road in the parking lot. She was furious and slapped me. It didn't compare to the right hook you gave me last week though. I haven't crossed paths with her since and hope to God I never see her again. These past two weeks have been the worst in my life." Connor stroked her cheek and tucked a loose strand of dark, silky hair behind her ear.

"It sounds cliché, but I've fallen so desperately in love with you, and it hurts more than anything I've ever experienced thinking I've lost you. Blowing out my knee and leaving the NFL hurt my body and my ego, but losing you, Meg, baby, has been eating me up inside. Please say you forgive me. That you believe me. I need you so much." He stroked her hair and kissed her.

It was a kiss of remorse, forgiveness, love, and Meg swallowed it up. She didn't need time to ponder, to digest what he said. Call her foolish, but she believed him and missed him terribly.

Meg reluctantly pulled away, wiping tears from her eyes. "I guess I owe you an explanation too."

"No, I made some assumptions. It's gonna be hard on the ego to accept that your best friend is a guy. Even if he is..."

"Gay? Tracy and I met my freshman year in college. We were lab partners, and he was the worst student I ever tutored. All he cared about was fashion and makeovers. The only reason he signed up for anatomy and physiology was because he thought he'd get to ogle naked men." Meg laughed through her tears as Connor grimaced. "We were both oddballs, and we clicked. I became his working model when he was trying out new fashion designs. Next thing I knew, I had a new hairdo, a shopping buddy and someone to show me the *right* way to dress. Apparently, dressing like the Amish was totally out. He helped out a lot with Emma too. Tracy is an amazing man. He may look totally superficial, but he taught me a lot about the importance of feeling good about myself. It's never really been about the clothes, but representing myself in a way I want to be viewed and feeling good about who I am."

"I'm glad you have him as a friend, Meg. Really."

"Me too. I miss him. He's the only one I ever confided in...before you, and it took two bottles of wine and a quart of ice cream to get it out of me."

"So I should be honored it only took four months of my constant pressure for you to confide in me?" he teased.

"Thank you for not giving up on me." She turned her lips toward his and breathed in his kiss, running her hands up and down his back, anxious to caress him, needing to touch him. His hands trailed down her spine, hers wandered under his sweatshirt and made contact with his hard, flat stomach.

Within seconds, he had her on her back and straddled her as his hands and mouth constantly moved over her inviting body.

"God, Meg. I want you so bad." He nipped her ear and trailed kisses down her neck. "I've missed you so much."

"You know, I hear make-up sex is amazing," she moaned.

Connor sat up, still straddling her, and raked his hands over his face. "Shit. Meg, I didn't mean to lose control." He rolled off her and helped her to a sitting position. "I didn't come here to have sex with you."

"Ouch. So now I understand how you've felt all these months when I've turned you down."

"No, no, no, no. Babe, there's nothing I want more than to make love to you, but not this way."

"Oh, I guess I'm kind of inexperienced—"

"Oh, honey." He cupped her face and kissed her lightly on the lips. "You're perfect. I don't want our first time to be make-up sex. We'll have plenty of time for that later. I want your first time to be an experience you'll always remember."

"Well, it's funny you say that." Meg shimmied out from under him and removed a manila folder from her briefcase. "Here." She handed the folder to him.

"What's this?"

"I had planned on surprising you with this two weeks ago but…well, stuff happened." She bit her lip and smoothed out her shirt while he flipped through the papers.

"The Colony Hotel? You made hotel reservations? For us?"

"Yeah," she said shyly.

"I've never been, but I hear the rooms are pretty nice. Ocean view. Jacuzzi in some rooms. You didn't cancel the reservations after…after what I pulled?"

"No, I forgot, and then I guess I sort of hoped things would work out. Do you have plans? I can change the date. Or cancel. Whatever—"

He cut her off with another knee-wobbling kiss. "Don't you dare cancel that room. I've got big plans for tomorrow night and you're the star attraction."

As promised, Connor picked her up right after breakfast. It was pure torture saying goodbye to him last night, but he said he needed to get some schoolwork done before they left for the weekend. Her overnight bag packed light as he requested. The emerald satin gown didn't take up too much space, and she didn't need too many spare clothes for tomorrow. She packed and repacked the few items struggling to subdue her quivering nerves.

Breaking the news to Emma turned out to be easier than she expected. Of course, her daughter gleamed with excitement but also blushed with embarrassment when she realized her mother would be having sex. "Use protection. Although, I wouldn't mind having a little brother or sister."

"Emma! I never said…" she stopped before she made herself look like an idiot. She was going away for the weekend, staying in a hotel with a man. Of course her daughter would assume—correctly—she was going to have sex. But it wasn't a topic she cared to talk about. They had the sex talk numerous times about Emma not having sex until she was thirty. Or married. Or at least not until she was with a man for a long time and truly loved him. The last thing she wanted was for her daughter to make the same mistakes she made.

Meg no longer lived in the dark ages. She knew her daughter wasn't a virgin and had slept with some of her past boyfriends. Emma had confided in her mother after she'd had sex with her boyfriend on prom night. Meg never got to experience prom or homecoming or first time jitters. Until now.

"Nervous?" Connor stroked the back of Meg's hand with his thumb as he backed out of her driveway.

Ha! Understatement of the year. "No," she lied turning her flushed cheeks from his view and taking in the landscape. There was less snow as they neared the Atlantic and drove south on Route 1. Maine blended into New Hampshire until you hit the coast.

Connor's hand only left Meg's when he needed to turn, and then he quickly picked up her hand again, setting it on his thigh. They talked about the weather, her grandparents, and Emma. He told her more stories about Cole and Mason and promised to have a family gathering soon. The three-hour drive seemed like mere minutes.

The Colony Hotel looked just like the images on the computer. The clear, blue water and white capped waves made a beautiful backdrop, even on a cold March day like today. Large bay windows lined the first floor of the hotel, each revealing a picturesque landscape of the beach or flowering bushes beginning to push out their tiny buds of rhododendrons, lilacs, and azaleas. Walkways wound through the newly pregnant shrubbery; white benches placed strategically at each bend, offering guests a place to rest or couples a private bench to enjoy a romantic moment together.

Meg checked them into their room while Connor brought in the bags. They remained quiet in the elevator and in the hallway. Before she inserted the key card into the door, he put the bags down and turned her toward him tenderly touching her cheek.

"I love you. You realize that, don't you?"

"I wouldn't be here if I didn't know it," she joked in an attempt to lighten the moment. He picked up the bags and she slid the key into the lock. She still hadn't said those three magical words to him and planned on doing so tonight. Sex and love were simultaneous in her book; tonight she would give and receive both.

The room was spacious and elegant. A plethora of fluffy white pillows and thick blankets covered the bed. Dark cherry furniture and black granite adorned the rest of the room making a dramatic, romantic, yet masculine, room. Meg opened the curtains to the balcony revealing the same million-dollar view of the Atlantic. "Wow. It's gorgeous."

"Mm, I couldn't agree more," Connor said as he came up behind her nuzzling her neck and wrapping his arms around her.

His touch warmed her yet created shivers down her arms and tingles in her belly. There was no doubt in her mind she loved him. For the first time in her life, she felt truly safe with a man. She covered his arms with hers and leaned into his powerful body, enjoying the soothing rhythm of the crashing waves in front of her and the strong beating heart behind her.

Minutes passed as they both stood in comfortable silence. Needing to feel more of him, Meg turned around and faced Connor. She reached up, pulling him closer as she kissed him slowly and passionately, showing him how much he meant to her.

Kissing Connor was like nothing she'd ever experienced before. The traumatic experience that led to her pregnancy was as far from romantic as a hot dog is gourmet cuisine, and her experimental make out session with Tracy back in her college days was a far cry from a toe curling experience. He'd wanted to deny his sexuality and thought kissing his best friend would straighten him out, and she'd believed kissing the one man in her life whom she truly felt at ease with would cure her from her fear of intimacy, but they were both wrong. Tracy remained gay, and Meg continued to fear men.

But Connor's kisses weakened her knees, melted her muscles, and heated up the depths of her soul.

She moaned.

He moaned.

He broke away. "Don't rush me babe, or we'll miss dinner and never leave the room."

She licked her lips and raised her perfectly groomed eyebrow. "So?"

Connor tilted his head and looked at her questioningly and hopeful.

"Why don't we order room service…later?" She tried to hide her schoolgirl smile, but it escaped from her swollen lips. Meg freed herself from his embrace and picked up her bag. "I'll be right out," she said as she slipped into the bathroom.

This wasn't what Meg had envisioned. She'd planned to have a romantic candlelit dinner, a walk under the stars, and then maybe a soak in the tub. But she couldn't wait any longer. Her entire adulthood, she had waited for the right man to come along. She'd told Tracy and Emma she didn't need a man, and for a long time Meg actually believed it. She believed needing and relying on anyone was a sign of weakness.

Well, one thing was for sure: Connor was her weakness. Smiling at her reflection in the bathroom mirror and taking in her sexy, yet modest lingerie, she'd have to admit having Connor McKay as a weakness wasn't too shabby. Taking one last breath to calm her tumultuous nerves, she reached for the handle and pulled open the bathroom door.

Connor turned and gasped. His beautiful baby blues stared at her for a long time before his gaze left hers to roam up and down her body. She was covered almost head to toe. Well, cleavage to toe with the exception of mile high legs breaking up the sea of green, but the intensity in his stare and the stiffness in his posture told her the silky investment was worth every penny.

"Wow."

While she wanted to make the first move, her feet felt heavy and refused to budge. She remained on the other end of the room, nervously toying with her ring and biting her lip.

"Come here." He sighed.

Slowly, she took a few steps. When she was within reach, he held out his hands and stroked his fingers lightly down her arms. "Damn, you're beautiful," he said keeping his eyes locked on hers. She stepped reluctantly closer and stared down at her feet.

"Look at me."

She complied, blinking constantly, afraid he'd see through her insecurities. She wasn't afraid of him, but of herself. Of taking the next step.

"Hey." He wiped a tear that fell from the tip of her long lashes. "What's wrong?"

"I want tonight to be perfect and I…I…I'm afraid of messing it up."

He smiled tenderly at her and kissed away the other tear that dripped involuntarily. "You relax and let me take care of you. You trust me, right?"

She nodded. "I do but I…I don't like being vulnerable."

"Shh." He pulled her body gently into his and gently stroked her back until she relaxed into him. He led her to the bed and pulled back the covers. "We don't have to do anything but lay here," he said as she slid beneath the white comforter. Climbing over her, he gazed into her eyes. "Baby." Connor stroked her cheek with the back of his fingers. "You say the word and we stop. I promise."

Meg closed her eyes and nodded. "Okay." But she didn't want him to stop. The heat from his body felt too nice. His touch the perfect amount of tenderness and strength. And his lips…Meg sighed. Those beautiful lips knew just how to kiss her into oblivion until she melted into a pool of warm chocolate.

Connor rolled off her and turned on his side before reaching to pull Meg closer to him. The rough texture of his hands gliding up and down her exposed arms sent tingles to places she had only read about. Goosebumps peppered her flesh as he trailed kisses down her neck. This was it. Her body was primed and ready for him. She picked up her limp arms and explored the corded muscles of his shoulders and back. Connor's body stiffened and then relaxed, pulling her in even closer.

Finally, he touched his lips to hers. "You're perfect," he murmured against her mouth.

Meg snorted. "Hardly."

Connor pulled back and stared before laughing. "Did you just snort?"

Her cheeks flushed, she bit her lip and made a poor attempt to hide her grin. "I believe you're hearing things."

"I don't think so." Connor quickly pinned her beneath him and started tickling her sides. "You're a snorter. I never would have believed it."

"I. Am. Not," Meg giggled and tried to wrestle free. They laughed and wrestled as he continued to tickle her sides.

Connor trapped her legs under his when she started to kick at him, then pulled her hands above her head with one of his and tickled her ribs even more.

Tears started to form in her eyes when she called out, "Stop. Connor, stop."

"Shit." Connor leaped out of bed. "Meg. I'm sorry. I didn't even think about it."

Shocked, Meg sat up in bed and took in the scene. Connor stood on the far end of the room, fully clothed and still aroused, pacing back and forth and avoiding looking at her. He leaned his forehead against the window and apologized again.

And then she figured it out. He thought she wanted him to stop. Well, she did. But stop tickling, not stop making love. So lost in the moment, enjoying the seriousness and the silliness of being with Connor, she didn't once think about her past. Instead, she focused on the future. By now the image of her being helpless and afraid was sketched in Connor's head. And she needed to erase it.

Slipping out of bed, she rushed toward Connor and hugged him from behind, resting her hands on his belly and her head on his back. "Connor. I'm okay."

"No you're not. I'm sorry. I shouldn't have trapped you like that."

Meg slid around his body so she was between the window and Connor. "Look at me. Do I look scared?"

Connor stared at her, remorse etched in the fine lines on his face. She smiled up at him and touched his lips with her fingers. "I'm okay. But I'll be even better if you come back to bed. And get naked."

"Really?"

Nodding, Meg pushed at his chest until he started walking backward toward the bed. Giving him one more push so he fell back on the mattress, Meg climbed up on him and kissed him. It felt wonderful to initiate the kisses and the touches. "I love you, Connor." Moaning, she kissed him deeper. "Make love to me, please."

All that karma crap his mother believed in must have been wearing off on him. Connor McKay, high school stud, former NFL running back, coach of the year and notorious ladies' man did *not* believe in fate, destiny, or soul mates. So why did one night of amazing sex turn him into a lovesick puppy?

He'd had sex before. Lots of times with lots of

women. Sex with Meg turned him all mushy inside. Why the hell didn't it totally freak him out? He was falling for her. Hell, he already fell so hard his head ached. There was no doubt in his mind he loved Meg Fulton. She was all he wanted in a woman. Not that he ever thought about it before. After the divorce, he pretty much put a halt to anything serious and had no desire to attempt to have a relationship with a woman.

But Meg changed him. She challenged him, tested him, taught him, and definitely pleased him. She loved him despite his hang-ups. *Okay, so maybe being an arrogant, cocky son-of-a-bitch isn't a hang-up.* But she loved him anyway. Not for his money or status, but for him. It sounded girly, that he liked that she loved and liked him for who he was. And he loved her. Every sexy, tasty, delectable inch of her.

Stroking the long, dark curls cascading over his chest and arm, and feeling the warmth from Meg's naked body on his relaxed him and totally turned him on. Usually after a session—because he didn't believe in overnights with his dates—of wild sex with a woman he'd be anxious to pull up his pants and bolt. Tonight, however, he couldn't imagine pulling himself away from the sleeping beauty at his side. Granted they were three hours away from home and pretty much stranded at the hotel for the night, which was all part of the plan. Twenty-four straight hours of uninterrupted time together.

So why the hell were they wasting it with sleep? Connor picked up the delicate yet strong hand curled on his chest and kissed each finger. He trailed his kisses up Meg's arm and into the crook of her neck.

She moaned.

He moaned.

And he showed her once again just how much she meant to him.

Chapter Fifteen

Spring in New England was always unpredictable. One day the sun would be out encouraging little buds to grow on trees and prompting spring bulbs to bloom—New Englanders would break out the Capri's and open toed shoes—and the next day would bring an onset of snow showers, winter coats, and snow scrapers.

The temperature may have vacillated during March and April, but the budding emotions between Connor and Meg steadily rose. They found it hard to keep their relationship a secret, but they didn't announce to the world they were sleeping together. Emma giggled and rolled her eyes when her mother blushed every time Connor came over, but she kept her word and didn't broadcast the affair.

Annie had reassured Meg that as long as she and Connor kept their relationship out of the job, it wasn't against school policy. Connor was tenured and since Meg and Jim both completed teacher observations and evaluations, Jim added Connor to his caseload. He had been hired as department head before she came to the district, so there was no favoritism there, but if another one of his department members wanted to apply for the position, she would not be allowed to be a part of the decision making. They still weren't comfortable advertising their relationship, but knowing it wasn't against school policy helped alleviate much of the angst Meg had been feeling.

Spring also meant less time with Connor. His afternoons and evenings were busy coaching baseball, but Meg was actually grateful for his hectic schedule. She lost all self-control and time-management skills when he loomed around her. Paperwork she normally would have done the moment it crossed her desk took an extra day to complete; household chores went undone so she could have a quick rendezvous with Connor.

Recently most of their quick conversations centered on J.T., one of his football friends from Texas. Every Memorial Day weekend he came up and stayed with Connor. He and his friends and family all looked forward to the annual visit.

J.T. was a celebrity in the football world—a world Meg never had an interest in, but since it was part of Connor's life, she had accepted it. He shared stories of his and J.T.'s days playing football in Texas. J.T. still played in the NFL, and Meg could tell Connor missed it and wished to be in his best friend's shoes. She cuddled with him while he told his stories, even if she had a hard time following along.

The two men sounded like complete opposites, and she assumed that's what drew the best friends together. She and Tracy had nothing in common except a profound respect and love for each other, and she figured that's what J.T. and Connor had as well.

She had an easier time following along with baseball than football. Eventually she learned the game while watching the team—or rather the coach—from the bleachers. Emma still worked part-time for the school covering softball and the girl's lacrosse team.

Connor's Memorial Day barbecue turned out to be more than a simple backyard affair. They had the traditional burgers, hot dogs, and steak. Potato and macaroni salad made by the wives of fellow friends, coaches, and family. Coolers overflowed with beer and soda. Classic rock bellowed from the CD player.

A group of men started a touch football game in the far corner of Connor's property, while Emma and Paige tossed horseshoes down by the lake and the women milled around the patio sipping on wine coolers and laughing at their husbands' showmanship. The property was large enough to accommodate a dozen more people and their cars, the lake making a beautiful backdrop.

This is what Meg had always wanted for her and Emma. To be part of a community that builds people up and takes care of each other when in need.

The buzz around J.T.'s arrival monopolized the conversation around school and among Connor's family. He was a celebrity the men envied and the women licked their lips at. They talked incessantly about the man's perfect, athletic body, and his mesmerizing blue eyes. Meg smiled and appreciated the lust that filled the women's eyes when they talked about J.T., but she couldn't imagine anyone in the world more perfect than Connor.

When the chips disappeared, she picked up the giant shell-shaped bowl and brought it into Connor's kitchen to refill. She looked out the kitchen window and admired the close-knit community. They came together in good times and in bad. She witnessed it last month when the Welker family's house burned down. Three children and a single mom suddenly homeless. The Tucker family offered them one of their unrented homes to live in—rent free—until they could get their feet back on the ground. Students brought in bags of clothing and toys for the little ones and local church groups rotated bringing homemade meals.

It was a community and Meg felt part of it. She and Emma babysat the young children while Diane went to various appointments with the insurance agency, builders, and banks.

Lost in nostalgia, she didn't hear the feet on the stairs and jumped when two strong arms wrapped around her stomach.

"Hey, gorgeous," Connor whispered as he nibbled on her ear.

"Mm, hey yourself." Meg let go of the chips and turned into his strength. Meeting his best friend was important to both of them, but it made her nervous. She hadn't had to worry about anyone's acceptance yet because the only people that saw them together were his family and a few teachers from school with whom she felt comfortable. J.T. was a part of Connor's life and Meg felt like a stranger, the newcomer. His acceptance was imperative. "You're pretty excited to see your BFF, huh?"

He chuckled. "BFF? Now you sound like my students. Yeah, I'm pretty pumped. J.T. and I haven't gotten together since August. I usually make a trip down to Texas in February but…" He gazed down at Meg's mouth and licked his smirking lips.

"Couldn't tear yourself away from me?"

"Damn straight. It's gonna kill me not being with you tonight. Are you sure you won't change your mind?"

She rested her head on his chest and sighed. "I'm not quite ready for a slumber party. I love waking up next to you in the morning, but I don't want to come downstairs and share my morning with a strange—with your friend."

Connor hugged Meg tighter, then released her and picked her up onto the counter nestling himself between her legs. Meg rested her arms on his shoulders and leaned her forehead against his. "When all of this is over—baseball, school, visits from out-of-town—we'll schedule some serious alone time. Okay?"

"Another sleepover? It's been a while."

"Hmm, if I didn't know better I'd say you were using

me for my body," she teased.

"Oh yeah, that and a whole lot more, babe." Connor kissed her and pulled her body into his until they melded into one. Meg wrapped her legs around his waist and enjoyed how beautiful and wanted he made her feel. She was so caught up in his kiss that she didn't hear the front door open, but the deep, bellowing voice was hard to ignore.

"Well, holy shit, Conman. Whatcha got cookin' in here?"

Meg pulled away and jumped off the counter using Connor's six feet frame to shield her from embarrassment. When he stepped away from her, she turned her back to the men and toyed with the chips on the counter, all while trying to cool the redness of her cheeks.

"J.T.! How the hell are you? How's the team?" She heard a clash of hands and backslapping as the two friends had their male ritual bonding moment.

"Sweet, man. Team's lookin' good this year. Could be the year for us. This the broad?"

Broad. Connor wasn't an eloquent man, but at least he wasn't brutish like his friend. Meg cleared her throat, anticipating their introduction and smiled as she turned around.

Connor walked back to Meg and put his arm possessively around her. "J.T., this is Meg. Meg, J.T."

She wiped her sweaty palm on her shorts. "Hi—" she looked up and faltered. The women were right. Those baby blue eyes were not eyes one could ever forget. They twinkled back at her as the blood left her face and made her weak. She gagged, swayed, ran into the bathroom, and threw up the three chips she ate earlier.

The cold, white porcelain did nothing to absorb the sweat leaking out of her pores. Meg stood on shaky legs and washed her mouth out in the sink.

"Hey, Meg, you okay?" Connor opened the unlocked

door and brushed her hair behind her ear. "Honey?"

Trembling lips. Spinning room. Nauseous stomach. Connor McKay. J.T. God. She wanted it all to stop.

She braced her hands on the counter hoping it could bear her weight. "I have to go," she whispered.

"It's okay. Come on. I'll help you up to my room."

"No. No," she shook her head. "I have to go. Home. Now." Meg straightened herself, blinked back tears, and pushed her way past Connor. He stayed next to her, offering a supportive arm around her waist, for which she was secretly grateful. Being a small, honest town, Meg, like everyone else in the community, left her keys in her car. She opened the driver's side door, but Connor stepped in the way.

"Hey, what's going on? You're not driving like this."

"I have to." He didn't move, and she knew he would fight her on it. "Emma. Please. Go get Emma." She pleaded. The weight of fear pushing down on her chest, suffocating her.

"Meg. Stop. What the hell is going on? One minute you're fine, and the next you're white as a ghost and throwing up. You need to lie down. Or a doctor. Do you need to go to the hospital? Are you pregnant?"

"What? No. Connor. Listen. Please. Get Emma. She can drive me home. But I need to leave. Now."

"I'll get Emma, but only because I don't want you driving yourself, and you're too stubborn to tell me what the hell is going on. Stay. I'll be right back." He stroked her cheek and ran around the house to the backyard.

Meg was thankful for the time to pull herself together before Emma got a look at her. She slid around to the passenger's side, knowing too well that Connor was right and she was in no condition to drive. She smoothed her hair back and fixed her rumpled T-shirt.

"Mom! Are you okay?"

"I'll be okay, sweetie. I'm not feeling well. Can you

drive me home?" She plastered on the motherly smile all moms used when they didn't want their precious children to be scared.

Connor opened her door, kneeled down in the dirt driveway, and then took her hand. "I'll come by in a little bit to—"

"No, Connor. Really. I just need to lie down. I'll call you later." Once again she showed her *I'm not really okay but I want you to think I am* smile.

He kissed her knuckles and backed away from the car.

Once home, Meg threw up again and again, then stripped down and took a hot shower and climbed into bed, shivering with fear. During the car ride, she tried to explain to her daughter that she had some flu bug, and she needed Emma to stay close. Just in case. She knew nothing would happen, but she needed her daughter to stay home as well. To stay far away from J.T. Spiller.

Emma seemed a bit miffed about missing the barbecue, but she'd have to get over it. This was for her own protection. Not that she'd understand it today. Or tomorrow. In the meantime, Meg curled into a fetal position and shook like a seven-point-five on the Richter scale. She barely managed to compose herself in front of Connor and Emma. Now that she was alone, the hurt, fear, and pain swallowed her up and closed in around her.

For a few brief months, she had the luxury of living a fairy tale life. And like all good things, it had to come to an end. How could she tell Connor that his best friend, the man whom he idolized, raped her and was the father of her child?

"Shit." Connor chucked his cell phone across his room and punched the back of the hardwood, six-panel door, bruising his knuckles.

Four days after her sudden onset of some sort of stomach bug, and Meg still hadn't returned any of his calls or texts. No one answered her door, yet her car remained parked in the driveway. She'd stayed home from work for the first time all year. He'd been so wrapped up with J.T.'s visit and then an away game in Concord that he hadn't found any time to catch up with Meg. He needed to find out why she was ignoring him.

How they could go from practically-having-sex-on-his-counter to leave-me-the-hell-alone in a matter of seconds was beyond him. If his schedule didn't suck so much, he'd be at her door demanding to be let in. Being the property owner, he had a key to the house and would use it tonight if she still refused to talk him.

During the first twenty-four hours of unreturned phone calls, he figured he'd called at bad times. She was sleeping. In the shower. But when Monday rolled around and still no word from her, he had begun to worry. Connor showed up on her doorstep at the crack of dawn. Emma answered the door and convinced him Meg had a bad case of the flu and needed to rest, but she still could have called him back.

J.T.'s short visited had been plagued with Connor's worry. They'd drunk the customary case of beer and stuntman shots of Southern Comfort at the picnic. Belched, farted, wrestled, and acted like caveman as usual. Connor was secretly happy Meg hadn't been there to witness his inner, drunken adolescence come out. It wasn't a side of him he was terribly proud of, but he didn't mind getting reckless every now and then.

He'd spent a leisurely Sunday on the deck, out on the boat, slowly sipping beers and grilling dogs with J.T. but he missed Meg.

"Man-up, Con. You're sorry ass is whipped!"

He'd brushed off the taunts but couldn't help the smirks whenever J.T. mentioned his hot girlfriend. Or when J.T. had pointed out that the Conman was in love. Damn straight. Which made the deafening silence from Meg unbearable. What if she had passed out? Was in a coma? Had fallen and couldn't get up? What if she needed him but couldn't get a hold of him?

It was the last thought which made him crawl on his hands and knees in search for his cell phone. He found it next to a fallen post-it note.

You are amazing.

Love you. M—

Connor closed his eyes and sighed. Meg had left that note on his pillow two weeks ago. She came over for dinner, but they had skipped dinner and went straight to bed. Well, the bedroom. She'd slipped out when he fell into his post-coital slumber.

He had waited her out. Given her whatever space Emma eluded she needed. But enough was enough.

Baseball practice had been long and excruciating, and his foul mood and his team whining about the unexpected heat wave New England was experiencing put him over the edge. The heat the sun produced was minor compared to the sauna that had built up inside his head. Steam from every mixed emotion under the sun cooked, baked and burned him until he had flipped out at his team and sent them home to take a cold shower.

He took his own advice as well. His skin felt refreshed, but the cold water didn't help soothe his heart. The lonely shower stall only made him reflect on the times he and Meg made love under the steamy flow.

Not caring about respect or boundaries, Connor shoved the post-it note and his cell phone in his pocket, stomped down the stairs, and then scooped up his car keys from the counter. Whether she liked it or not, she would talk to him and tell him what the hell was going on.

Aerosmith and the white-knuckle death grip on the black leather steering wheel didn't help calm his nerves.

And why did his nerves need calming? There were no signs that their relationship was in trouble, but Connor sensed it. He knew.

The truck practically lead itself to Meg's driveway, and his legs followed suit by delivering him to her front door. Her car sat in the driveway and a light shined through the living room window. He heard voices inside. Possibly the television or radio. There was hope. He took one final deep breath and rang the doorbell.

The voices stopped. Connor leaned in and pressed his cheek against the door hoping to hear her, touch her. The door opened taking Connor's face with it causing him to literally fall at Meg's feet. Beautiful feet. Bright pink polish, smooth silky legs. He lifted his head and took in her beauty. Struggling with emotion and wobbly knees, he lifted himself up and loomed over her. But the flawless face, pouty lips, and large doe eyes were gone.

"Oh my God! Meg. Babe. You look awful."

She laughed a humorlessly, "You have no idea," she whispered and turned away from him.

Shit. Cancer. It was cancer. She was dying right before his eyes. Maybe it was a tumor. A brain aneurysm.

"Honey, sit down. Should I call your doctor?" He grabbed her hand and pulled her to the couch. Once sitting, he inspected her face with his hands, the need to touch her pulling at his aching body. Her skin felt like porcelain, but her eyes were sunken and outlined with dark circles. She always looked thin, but she'd lost a few pounds. Carefully he drew her close to him and held her and kissed her hair as he stroked her back.

She was wound up tighter than a rookie on opening day. Connor pulled back, his hands gripping her shoulders. "What is it?"

She squeezed her eyes shut, but the tears leaked through the barrier anyway. "Connor. I…we need to take a break from each other."

"What?" This time he was the one who let out a humorless laugh.

She opened her eyes and pulled away from his grasp. "This all happened so fast, and while it's been wonderful, it just doesn't feel right anymore."

"It sure the hell felt right last week when we were making love on my couch."

Meg jumped up and hugged her arms around her waist. "It was…nice. Yes. But we need to stop now. I need us to stop now."

Connor cornered her in front of the fireplace and scowled down at the senile woman before him. "What the hell are you talking about? Are you out of your freakin' mind?"

"Please, Connor." She stepped back as far as she could before bumping into the fireplace. The fear in her eyes was enough to make Connor back down and step back. He was pissed at her, but he didn't want to frighten her.

"I need my space. You're a wonderful man but not for me. Not right now."

"Again, I repeat, are you out of your freakin' mind? Things are great with us." A light went on in his head and he smirked his *I can talk a woman into anything* smirk. "J.T. didn't put you up to this, did he? Before he left, he told me he planned on stealing you away from me."

"No!"

Her sudden burst of energy startled him.

Meg ran her hand through her hair, straightened out her oversize T-shirt. "Please. Connor. Just go."

Her passivity made his anger boil. They were a fighting couple. She was an aggressive woman. There was no way their relationship would go down without a fight. "I won't go until you tell me what the hell is really going on. Don't tell me the rumor-mill has come up with some lame ass story about—"

"No, Connor," she sighed. "I don't want to hurt your feelings, but if you must know, it's because of who you are."

"I thought you were past that athlete fetish."

"No, I mean, you're…you're a teacher in my school. I'm your boss, and I need to earn my respect without riding on your coattails."

"Sugar, you've got respect *despite* being secretly linked to me." Once again, he tried his trademark smirk.

Meg strolled to the front door and opened it. She picked her head up, straightened her shoulders, her face hardened.

"Frankly, Connor, I don't want to date a teacher. It isn't ethical for someone in my position. I'm a principal. And besides, I need my space. I feel crowded and claustrophobic. I'm used to being single and have missed my freedom. Now please leave. No hard feelings of course." She smiled her smug smile that he knew so well. The, *I'm the boss. This is how it will be done. Suck it up and do what I say* smile.

Connor slammed the door, remaining inside. The force knocking a picture off the wall shattering the glass. He wasn't a violent man but provoked, he didn't back down. Ever. Meg had gotten under his skin before and she encountered his temper on many occasions, but tonight would be the first time she saw the red-hot tempered Connor. He gripped her shoulders until she looked up at him.

"You are not dumping me because I'm a *teacher.* The irony, babe, is classic. You got freaked out, and now you're cowering in your secret hole. Not gonna fly. Now what the hell is going on?"

She rolled her shoulders and winced. At his words or the grip, he wasn't sure. He didn't want to hurt her. Slowly he loosened his grip and bit back the flow of curse words he really wanted to utter. Meg didn't look away.

Her dark eyes bore into him, but she didn't speak. Her face hid any emotion. She was serious; she was dumping him. All these years he had hoped to find someone to appreciate the real him, not the NFL player or brief stint of fame that followed him around, but the smart, loyal, family-orientated, hardworking Connor McKay. And the irony of it all was that it wasn't enough. At least that's what Meg Fulton told him.

"You had no problem sleeping with the teacher. Telling the teacher how much you loved him. Something happened. Someone made an off-base comment, and you're jumping to conclusions." Connor loomed over her and inwardly cringed when she sunk her head into her shoulders and backed away in fear. "I'll back off for now, but I'm not done with you, Meg Fulton. This is a bunch of bullshit fear, but I'll give your space. For now."

After a minute of intense silence, the sound of his heavy breathing the only noise in the room, Connor yanked the front door open and slammed it, shutting the door on his past, present, and future.

The frame holding the Warren Kimble print was still intact, but the glass had shattered. Just like her life. Slowly Meg slid down the wall, cradled her knees, and wept. And wept. And wept. She hurt him, which wasn't what she wanted to do, but he wouldn't accept her need for distance. Connor could always see right through her.

For the past few days, she ran through excuses she could use to end the relationship. *Emma really needs all of my attention. I'm in love with another man. Tracy isn't gay, and we have realized we're destined for each other.* Connor wouldn't buy any of them, and he would have kept coming back. The only way to make him stay away was to hit his venerable spot.

Two days ago, she had changed her mind and decided

to call him and tell him the truth about J.T. Surely he would ditch his best friend, his only tie to the NFL community that he longed to be a part of, and devote the rest of his life to her: the insecure single-mother whom he despised months ago and had been recently sleeping with.

Pieces of previous conversations quickly came together. Connor mentioned having ties to friends in Manchester but never mentioned any names. Probably because he was sensitive to her past, knowing she had no friends growing up. He lived two hours away from the city yet had more friends than she did after spending fifteen years of her life there. It was only natural for two small town boys from New Hampshire who made it big in the NFL to become friends. How Meg could have been blind to that for the past few months could only be blamed on love. It truly blinded her from the harsh ironies in life.

Try as she may, Meg never revved up the nerve to call Connor. Hence his impromptu visit, her bitchy break up lines, and emotionless goodbye. Her days of mourning had to end. She needed him to believe what she said. That he was *beneath* her and she needed her independence back. And she needed to convince herself that she made the right decision.

Chapter Sixteen

Three weeks went by, and they had only crossed paths once. Meg had stopped attending baseball games. Connor was too busy coaching—and preparing for the state championship—to notice her anyway, so she told herself. But the final department head meeting of the year was unavoidable. Thankfully, eight other department leaders were there as well. She smiled, congratulated each department on their success with the new initiatives, and gave final preparations for the end of the year, final exam schedule, and graduation practice and ceremonies. Connor sulked. She smiled and spat out a few—prepared in advance—jokes all in an attempt to appear "normal."

He didn't respond. She didn't expect him to. And now, with graduation behind her and the school quiet and empty, Meg could go to work relaxed, knowing the only people she would have to face were her secretary, assistant principal, and the superintendent. And not the man who filled her heart and soul with more love than she ever deserved. Not him because she had shoved that love back in his face, ripped his heart out, and fed it to the sharks.

He knew he was overstepping the boundaries,

crossing unchartered territory and possibly losing her trust, but Tracy had to follow his gut. And it told him Meg was making the biggest mistake of her life. Of course, it could all backfire and her worst fear could be thrown in her face: rejection. But Tracy truly believed when Connor heard the truth he'd ditch that womanizing bastard he called best friend and run straight into the arms of his true love.

Yes, Tracy was a sucker for fairy tales and Happily Ever Afters.

He'd always been a romantic. Just because Tracy's love life was in the crapper didn't mean Meg's needed to be. His shoulders had housed her secrets, her fears, her tears for long enough. *Man up*. He rolled his shoulders and stepped out of his mini-coup. Yeah, it screamed *I'm gay!* If he expected Meg to face her fears, he couldn't exactly be the pot calling out the kettle. Connor McKay sounded like a good guy. He wouldn't beat the crap out of Tracy like the jocks did in high school. He hoped.

Maybe that was why he and Meg clicked so quickly in college. They both ran away from the same thing. The same fear. She thought he was the strong one in the relationship, little did she know he had been living vicariously through her for the past ten years. It was easy to come out of the closet in the fashion industry in New York. Hell, if he wasn't gay, he'd have faked it. No one would hire a male personal shopper who *wasn't* gay. But Meg had it tough. Single mom. No parents. Loving grandparents who raised her, but they had been old with one leg into the nursing home. She gave up everything for her daughter and fought like she was after the last Valentino in an after Christmas sale at Saks.

Pulling at the collar of his Ralph Lauren polo—he figured Brooks Brothers in rural New Hampshire in the middle of July would be overdoing it—and brushing the driving wrinkles out of his Diesel jeans—You can take the boy out of the fashion capitol of the east, but you can't take the style out of Tracy James!—Tracy marched confidently up the steps to Connor's house. He'd never been an outdoors kind of guy, but the fresh air and reflection of the sun off the lake did make him a bit nostalgic.

Before he could fold his fingers into a knocking fist, the front door swung open and the linebacker—or whatever he was—crashed into him and knocked his high-end ass on the porch and down the steps. Fashion school didn't offer training for rectifying an entrance like that one.

Connor pulled the buds of his iPod out of his ears. "Shit. Sorry. I didn't see you, man. I'm heading out for a run." He offered a big, calloused hand to Tracy and helped him to his feet with little effort. As dignified as he could, Tracy stood and wiped the country dirt off his designer jeans.

Tracy lifted his head and smiled. Recognition set in and Connor scowled. "I'm in no mood for a fashion make-over." He put the buds back in his ears and turned his iPod up. AC/DC's *Back in Black* cranked so loud Tracy's head started to vibrate. He braced himself for his next move and yanked the thin, white wires down, practically taking a piece of the alpha stud's ear with him.

"I have something I need to say and you will listen…dammit!" He didn't come off sounding as macho as he had hoped. Tracy was pretty sure whatever he said in the presence of the wall of testosterone in front of him would come out sounding wimpy.

Connor braced his thick hands on his hips and glared down at Tracy. "Make it fast, Armani."

Okay, Tracy would give him credit for name-dropping. "I, uh, wanted to tell you Meg had a really tough life growing up…" Connor continued to squash him with his glare so he fought hard to stand up taller.

"Pregnant at fifteen, early graduation, raising a kid by herself—"

"Tell me something I don't know." Connor swiped his iPod back.

"She's the best friend a guy or girl could ask for. She's completely selfless and has sacrificed a great deal in her life. Did you know she was valedictorian of her class…at Central High School? In Manchester, New Hampshire? Do you know what year she graduated? Anyone else in that class you know as well?" He prayed Connor could fill in the blanks. He had already betrayed Meg's trust by being here, but it wasn't like he exposed her secret—simply pointing Connor in the right direction. "I guess I'd better go. Thanks for listening."

Tracy kept his head held high as he race-walked to his tiny car. He didn't look back, afraid of what he might encounter. He'd be damned if Connor made the connection, damned if he didn't. The tires spun as he peeled out of the dirt drive and headed back to the safety of New York City.

Well, if that wasn't the strangest conversation he'd ever had. Connor wasn't even breaking a sweat as he jogged into his third mile. He usually turned around at the Dausey Dairy Farm, but he needed more than a six mile run today. AC/DC had segued into Nickelback's *"Rock Star."* He lived that life for five minutes and didn't think it was all MTV cracked it up to be. Visiting J.T. every year and reuniting with the NFL/Rock Star life didn't leave him wanting more, just wanting out. It suited his best friend, though. J.T. showed no signs of letting up his lifestyle. Easy girls, no drugs but enough alcohol in the off-season to make up for it, lots of parties, and no privacy.

Huh, he didn't envy that life. Pitied it. When J.T.

retired, he'd appreciate the small towns, home cooked meals, and nice girls. Or not. Hell, look what the *nice girl* did to him. Loved him and left him because he wasn't good enough. Maybe J.T. had the right idea. Connor had roots in small town America, J.T. was from New Hampshire as well, but at least he grew up in a city. From…Connor stopped in his tracks and stared blankly at the dairy cows and miles of endless pasture.

"Holy freaking cow shit." He spun around quickly and raced back to his house breaking every previous record he made rushing in the playoff game against San Diego. How the hell could he have been so stupid? The signs were there, all he had to do was read them. Why hadn't he ever asked Meg about her high school? Made her talk more about the asshole who raped her? Part of him wanted to believe it was because he loved Meg too much and didn't want her to ever think about her tragic past, but another part of him knew he avoided the conversation because it made *him* uncomfortable. Connor was an insensitive jackass. The need to right his wrong and end all ties to J.T. ran rampant through his veins. Anger swamped his body and pushed his legs faster. He needed to get home.

Drenched in sweat and breathing rapidly from anger, fear, and confusion—not from his six-minute miles—he dropped in front of his computer and looked up the phone number for American Airlines. He made a quick call, pulled out his American Express card, stripped, showered, and raced out to his truck peeling his tires the same way Armani had in his toy car less than an hour ago.

Rush hour traffic did little to slow him down. Weaving between slow-moving commuters, Connor made it to the airport in record time. With no luggage or carry-ons, he printed his ticket at the kiosk and jogged toward his terminal right before boarding time.

In no mood to converse, Connor made a grumpy seat

companion. He warded off the old lady's attempt to be friendly by closing his eyes, facing the window, and feigning sleep. Window seats weren't meant for men his size, but booking a last minute flight didn't give him much choice in seat selection, much less a cheap fare. You would figure an $800 flight from Manchester to Austin would provide a meal. His stomach growled, it obviously knew seven o'clock was time to refuel, but that would mean he'd have to open his eyes, ask for one of the ridiculously small packages of pretzels, and risk telling off the nice grandma to his left.

Instead, he opted for silence, sans the growling stomach. Skipping lunch in lieu of a workout and missing dinner to hop on a plane probably wasn't the smartest idea, but food was not a top priority. Solving the complicated web Tracy—he *did* remember his name—spun for him was more important.

Five hours later, the plane landed and the hot, sticky Texas air welcomed him. Hailing a cab, Connor spat out an address and stared out at the lights of the restless city. He didn't have a plan, hadn't figured out what he would say. It would come to him.

The cab pulled in front of the ritzy apartment complex and Connor tossed a wad of bills in the front seat. "Thanks," the cab driver yelled to his back.

Connor stormed through the wide, glass doors and barked at the overpaid employee behind the reception desk. "I need to go up to Penthouse C."

"Sir," she smiled politely, "Are you expected company?"

"No."

"Well, then, I'm sorry, but I'm under strict—"

"J.T. Spiller. Buzz him. Tell him Connor is here."

She stared at him, offended with his disrespect.

"Now!" he barked.

She huffed and slowly picked up the phone. Her

heavily made-up eyes looked down, and she blushed as she smiled shyly. "Now, Mr. Spiller…" J.T. was probably asking her what color panties she had on. She finally put the phone down and smiled, not so kindly, at Connor. "Mr. Spiller will see you now."

"No shit," he muttered. She directed Connor toward a private elevator, which opened to the Penthouse. It was only last summer that he rode the same elevator, laughing, drunk, and sweaty after a few passes with some of his old teammates. Tonight's sweat came from a different kind of adrenaline. It flowed like a freaking river.

After an eternity, the bell chimed and the doors opened to a showy suite. J.T. was surprisingly alone. "Hey, dude! This is a surprise! What the hell brings you to Austin? Are you and—" he was cut off with a sharp left hook to the jaw. J.T., taken by surprise, fell back to the wall.

Connor stormed past him and into the living room. "What the shit is all this about? Have you completely lost it?" J.T. strung an impressive line of curse words that would make a sailor blush and cornered Connor.

"Back off asshole."

"Me back off? You're crazy, Con. If I miss training this week because of a swollen eye—"

"You shouldn't have provoked me." His temper still raged, but he spoke quietly. Freakishly calm.

"Me? I opened the flippin' door!"

Connor took a step toward him, and his reflexes pushed J.T. back a few feet. "Your whole life you've been *messin'* around. Screwing up people's lives, taking advantage of them." He inched closer until they stood toe-to-toe. "Raping them."

J.T.'s head jerked. "Rape? You are drunk. High, whatever. I've never—"

"Don't lie to me, James."

"Dude, seriously. And what's with this *James* shit.

No one has called me that since high school."

Connor worked overtime, telling his blood to cool before it boiled over and he strangled the criminal in front of him. He gritted his teeth and skewered the asshole with his piercing stare. "This whole time…all these years…you've fooled me, man. But I swear, if you ever come near her, near me, near Emma, I will hunt you down and kill you."

"Who the hell is Emma? Dude, Connor, speak English. You're freaking me out. You come busting into my home and go ape-shit on me and accuse me of rape? *Rape?* Since when did I need to rape a girl?" he smirked, but Connor didn't smile back. "Dude, you're serious? Honestly, man. I—"

"Save it, asshole. I know about high school. You thought you could bury your dirty little secret—"

"High school?"

"Meg told me about you."

"Meg? Your girlfriend, Meg? I didn't know her in high school, much less do her. She's hot, man. I would have totally remembered bang—"

Connor lurched forward and grabbed J.T. by his T-shirt collar and pinned him to the wall. "Don't you dare." They stared at each other, sweaty and irritable, and J.T.'s dumbfounded expression added fuel to the fire.

"I've never laid a hand on her. I swear! I only met her once, and four seconds later she was hurling her lunch in your toilet!"

"You did more than lay your hand on her. You raped her and got her pregnant!"

"Dude! If you can't trust your girl, don't come blaming me. You never did get over your trust issues after Amy screwed you over."

"In high school, asshole!" Connor pinned J.T. into the wall again, forcing him to gasp for air. "You raped her in the back of your car and left her there while you continued to party."

"I didn't know her in high—" The realization struck, and J.T. went limp in his hands. "Four-eyes Fulton," he whispered. "Shit."

Connor dropped him and he slid to the floor. All this time, Connor had assumed Meg grew up in Boston where she'd been teaching before coming to Newhall. If Tracy hadn't pointed him in the right direction, he might never have learned she had actually grown up in the same town as J.T. It was another one of those *assume* things. Somehow the topic of her hometown name never came up.

Holding his head in his hands, J.T. slouched and breathed heavily. "Four-eyes Fulton we called her. She tutored us in math and science and shit. A genius kid. That night…at the party…I felt bad for her and hung out with her for a bit. I was drunk. High. I probably did acid. Shit, it was so long ago I don't really remember." He picked up his head and remained sitting on the floor. "I don't remember much from that night. We went to my car to fool around. I think I blacked out. I dunno. I remember waking up the next morning wondering if I was tripping or if we really did have sex in my car. She never said anything so I figured…figured I'd tripped out too much on the acid."

"You're a goddamn rapist. You took advantage of a young virgin and left her, a victim, in the backseat of your car. Left her to raise a child at the age of sixteen. Left her alone. And you're going to pay."

J.T. slowly stood, trembling on his weak knees and cradling his ribs. "She thinks I *raped* her?" He stared at Connor, soaking in the life-changing news bulletin. "She was pregnant? Her daughter, she's mine?"

"No. She'll never be yours. You promise me right here, right now, that you'll never go near either one of them. If you do, this will look like a slap on the back in comparison. Understand?"

"Yeah, yeah," he sighed.

Connor kicked the glass coffee table over and didn't even so much as flinch when the glass shattered across the hardwood floor and gave his former best friend a final look over.

His hand touched the doorknob when J.T. said his last words. "I didn't know, Con. I didn't know. I was a kid. Stupid. I swear, I didn't know."

Connor let the door slam behind him, closing out his past.

The flight back mirrored the flight to Texas except this time it was a nosey old man who chatted while Connor sulked. Connor didn't feel any better. Didn't feel any worse for wear, minus the swollen knuckles, dark circles under his eyes, and wrinkled clothes. Truth be told, he looked like a thug. He didn't notice the blood on his T-shirt until a security man called him out and brought him to a room to be searched and interrogated.

Like his mother's apple pie, New Hampshire greeted him with a sense of comfort. The city surrounding the airport was a ghost town. One of the perks of living in small town America was that all traffic lights turned to a blinking yellow system after midnight. Slow and cautious at every intersection instead of the stop and go traffic of a busy city like Austin, he cruised through the fourth light and noticed a twenty-four hour diner open for business. Remembering his growling stomach, Connor pulled in, found a table, and ordered the Lumberjack special. He ate slowly, his jaw a bit tight from the swelling pressure.

It was nearly two in the morning before he drove past the "Welcome to Newhall" sign. It didn't seem all too long ago that he was a teenager, sneaking girls down to the lake behind the sign hoping to score, or at least get on base. He hit a few grand slams in his day. Out of the park and down a girl's pants, but he never, ever took advantage of a girl. Ever.

He couldn't imagine how betrayed Meg had felt when he introduced her to J.T. Damn, he felt like a shmuck. But she had to realize he didn't know the truth. That he'd never ask her to face the guy who raped her. The shock was as startling to him as it was to her. In the morning he'd clear things up with her, make it all right. Hope she'd realize his error as pure ignorance and beg for her forgiveness.

White knuckling the steering wheel, he thought back to the look on J.T.'s face when he called him out on the rape. Connor's mind had been so focused on rage that it was too late by the time he noticed the headlights coming at his driver's side door. The sudden impact and crunching of metal against his body knocked him clear to the passenger seat even with the seat belt snugly fastened. Air bags deployed softening the blow to his head as it bounced off the headrest and toward the steering wheel. His ribs cracked like toothpicks and pierced his insides, sending him into a whirlwind of pain and a blackness of unconsciousness.

Chapter Seventeen

Emma was in high spirits lately, mostly because she enjoyed flirting with Connor's younger brother, Cole, while tending to the horses on the Tucker farm. Unfortunately, Meg couldn't avoid his family. Emma rode twice a week and worked for Betsy and George to supplement the fee of lessons. Annie had become one of Meg's closest friends and even though she meddled, Meg couldn't help but adore Betsy. To make Connor believe she didn't need him meant she had to keep up her act of living a completely happy life without him.

While they never publicly discussed their relationship, rumors around town buzzed about Meg and Connor's secret relationship and mysterious break-up. Sick of the pitying looks, she continued her happy-go-lucky façade at work as well.

Keeping true to her pretend world, she planted a smile on her face, opened the door to the main office, and then called out an over-the-top cheery "Good morning!" to Barbara. "Don't you just love mornings like these? Not too hot, not cold, not a cloud in the sky. What do you think about closing up shop and heading to the beach?"

Barbara had a deer in the headlights look. "I'm only teasing. And a tad bit wishful thinking. You ought to…Barb? Are you okay?" Her secretary didn't blink and a lonely tear trickled down her cheek. "Oh my God, what's wrong?" Meg dropped her briefcase and kneeled down so she was eye level with the stray tear.

"It's Connor McKay," she whispered.

The sharp pang in her chest clogged her airways for a second. "What about Connor?"

"An accident. He's—"

Meg shot up. "He's what?" she demanded.

"At Mercy. Critical care."

"Oh, God." Meg tripped over her briefcase and ran out the door to her car, breaking every speed limit on the way to the hospital.

Thankfully the parking lot wasn't too full, and she was able to park relatively close to the emergency room entrance. Besides a few minor stitches for Emma during her high school days, Meg had been fortunate enough to avoid hospitals. She didn't have a fear of them, but the sad and depressing air that loomed around the ominous brick buildings was enough to make her thankful for a healthy life.

Stale, antiseptic air enveloped her as she rushed through the heavy doors and approached the check-in desk. "Connor McKay. I need to see him. He was brought in…I don't know when, but I need to talk him," she begged.

The woman behind the desk eyed her up and down, scrutinizing Meg's appearance. "Are you a family member?"

"Um, no. A friend. But please, can you tell me if he's okay? Can you tell me that much? Is he okay?"

"Ma'am, I'm not at liberty to discuss a patient's diagnosis, prognosis, or condition with anyone, especially *friends.* Do you realize how many *friends* Mr. McKay has?"

"Please..." she looked for a nametag, "Carla. I'm his...girlfriend. Tell me he's okay."

Maggie guffawed. "Do you know how many *girlfriends* he's had stop in today?"

Taken aback by the woman—who couldn't be older than thirty—and her attitude, Meg lost control of her emotions.

"How dare you—"

"Meg! Oh, God. I'm so glad you're here!" Betsy wrapped her short, pudgy arms around Meg's shoulders and sighed.

Quickly she pulled away, "Connor, he's...?"

"He's a mess. Maybe seeing you will bring him back to...life. Room 237. I'm heading home to rest for a bit. I'm glad you're here. Go on in. I'll be back in a few hours." Betsy patted her on the back and slowly shuffled out the door.

Not waiting another minute, Meg pushed the up arrow on the elevator and waited impatiently for the doors to open. Once inside, she practiced a few yoga breaths in an attempt to calm her nerves. She had no idea what to expect. Barbara and Betsy were incredibly vague and evasive. Was it because they didn't know how to break it to her? Was he paralyzed? In a coma? Brain damaged?

Finally, the doors opened and she hurried down the hall to his room. As she started to pull on the door handle, a large elderly nurse walked out of his room.

"You're not going in there are you?"

"Uh, yes. If that's okay."

"Uh, uh. You're too frail for the likes of him. Sugar, why don't you come back later?"

Searching for a name again, she continued to hold on to the tiny thread of strength she had left. "Thank you, Florence, for your concern, but Connor is a friend of mine and I'd like to see him now."

"Huh. Well, sugar, good luck to you."

"Wha...what do you mean? Is he...terribly disfigured? On his death bed?"

Florence let out a growl, "Honey, if those injuries don't kill him, I'm sure as likely to go in there and smother him with a pillow myself." She waddled down the hall with a toss of her hand in the air.

The world was losing its sanity! First Carla treating her like paparazzi and then Betsy leaving to rest—*rest!*—when her son was dying, and then Florence, a nurse who should be fighting to keep her patients alive, threatens to kill Connor? Meg knew she had definitely missed something, and she hadn't the foggiest idea what it was. Bracing herself for the worst, she slowly opened the heavy door and reluctantly stepped closer to the hospital bed.

The room was dark and still except for the occasional drip from his IV. Connor lay flat on the bed, his shoulders bare and scraped, his ribs mummified with white bandages. The left side of his face had swollen to twice its original size and a purple bruise covered his cheek. His right side had tiny red cuts from his forehead down to his neck. The lump in her throat and the tightness in her chest kept her from running into his arms. Not that he could hold her with one arm weighed down with the IV. Or that she'd dare touch him. He looked defenseless. Weak. The only other time she saw him this vulnerable was the day she shot his Achilles' heel and kicked him out of her house.

Losing him had been the most painful emotion she had ever experienced, but if she lost him permanently, she didn't know what she would do. Maybe it was a mistake to break up with him. She lost a month of valuable time she could have spent with him, and now she'd never be with him again. Connor looked like death warmed over. He was strong, physically and mentally, but the way his nurse and mother talked…well, she didn't know if he would make it.

Inching closer, she leaned over his broken and bruised body and pulled the thin white blanket over his torso and tucked it under his chin and left her hand on the thin barrier, needing the contact.

"I told you to leave me the hell alone!" Connor opened his eyes and glared at her. "Meg?" His baby blues softened.

"Hi, I'm sorry…I didn't…you…uh, wanted to be alone. I'll go now." She turned and took a step, but he reached out and touched her lingering hand.

"Don't go," he whispered.

She slowly turned and faced him, keeping her eyes on his injuries and not his watchful stare. They stayed motionless in silence. His thumb brushed across her knuckles. She closed her eyes absorbing his touch, remembering his potency and how wrong she was for him. Reluctantly, she pulled away. "Are you okay? I mean, you look awful, but are you…are you going to be okay?"

Connor smirked his telltale grin, "Nah, this is nothing. A few scrapes. I've done worse."

"What happened?" She remained serious while he did his best to lighten the mood.

"Guy was multi-tasking. Sleeping and driving. He ran a light, hit me broadside. I have a few busted ribs, nothing major."

"Oh." Meg toyed with her ring and bit thoughtfully on her lower lip. "Your mother and the nurse said…I thought you were…" she bit back the tears in her throat. "Uh, not doing well."

"Well, if she'd stop manhandling me, I'd be doing a lot better."

"Isn't that sort of her job?"

As if on cue, Florence entered, wheeling a small portable stand that housed her necessary equipment.

"Time for your vitals, hot shot." She undid the Velcro on the blood pressure strap and pushed her way over to Connor's right side. "You may want to step outside for this, honey. He's a miserable bear."

"Just ignore Nurse Ratchet. She's getting grumpier in her old age." Connor's eyes remained fixed on Meg.

"And your morphine has obviously worn off. You're gonna start listening to me, or I'm going to dope you up again. Do I make myself clear?"

"Crystal. And do I make myself clear, Aunt Flo? No doping me up. I hate that sh—crap."

"I swear," Florence turned around and addressed Meg. "He's gotta be the most stubborn, obstinate man I've ever met. He won't wear a gown, won't take medication and thinks, *thinks* he's gonna get out of here tonight! Not on my watch." She turned back toward Connor. "And you, seriously, Connor. Two in the morning? Hasn't your mama taught you anything? Where are you coming from at such a god-awful time of night? You're lucky you didn't go and get yourself killed!"

"Oh, stop the melodrama. First off, I'm not wearing a sissy ass gown—"

"Watch your mouth, young man." Florence tore off the blood pressure strap and stuck a thermometer in his ear.

"And I don't need drugs. I feel fine!"

"Tough guy," she muttered and picked up his right hand, examining his swollen and bruised knuckles. "Funny how you got hit on the left side of your body but your right hand looks like it went through the wringer as well. You been fighting again?"

He jerked his hand free and grimaced. "If you're done with the third degree, you can go now. I remember you saying I need my rest if I'm going to get out of here."

Florence muttered as she packed up her rolling cart and strolled out of the room.

Meg crossed her arms and arched her eyebrow. "What the heck is going on? I feel like I'm in *The Twilight Zone*."

"She's Kent's mom." He rolled his eyes. "She was kind of like our nanny growing up. She and mom started the cleaning business together when Annie and I were kids. When mom was working, Flo watched us and we'd hang out with Kent. The old broad acts like a mother hen sometimes."

"Okay, so that makes a little more sense. I guess this is all a tough love act?"

Connor laughed. "Yeah, Aunt Flo always comes off harsh, but that's to cover up the fact she's a total softie."

"Well then, since you're okay, I'll leave you to rest." Meg eyed his bruised hand one more time, picked up her purse, and then walked toward the door.

"Meg. Thanks. For coming by."

"Sure."

She made it to the car before she burst into tears. It took a month for her to finally be able to wake up in the morning and not picture Connor the second her alarm clock went off. A month of extreme workouts in the gym, intense house cleaning and extra hours in her office all in an attempt to ward off any thoughts and images of Connor that may have crept into her mind

Now, after watching him lay helpless but still manly in his hospital bed, smiling and making jokes with Florence, she was totally, one hundred percent doomed. Carrying on with the charade of not loving him made her physically and mentally exhausted. Her body couldn't keep up with the act much longer. The brief contact he made was enough to set off the fire alarms throughout the hospital, yet he appeared unaffected. Sure, he stared at her and fidgeted, but after the way she treated him, what did she expect? He didn't profess his undying love to her or tell her he'd been brooding for the past month.

No, he was obviously coming home from some torrid affair when he had gotten into his accident. He'd moved on. And left her in the dust.

More rattled now than when he woke up from his brief stint of unconsciousness to four EMT guys using the Jaws of Life on his truck, the ache in his chest wasn't so much from his bandaged ribs, but from Meg's face. Truth be told, she looked awful. Beautiful, but thin, frail, and weak. He recognized her signs of nervousness. She wanted to appear strong and in full working order, but from word on the street—his mother and sister were quite handy when he needed information on Meg—was that she'd turned aloof and depressed, working very hard to come off as the strong, in charge woman she liked to be.

He still couldn't figure out how that made him feel. Last week, he secretly gloried that she was miserable for—what he thought—being a self-righteous pain in the ass. Connor would never utter those words to anyone else, but after the way she dumped him, that's what he'd thought of her. Learning she was miserable hadn't done much in the form of comforting him, but he'd been happy to know she wasn't out searching for her next victim.

But she wasn't self-righteous, and at times she could sure be a pain in the ass, but he loved that ass more than anything in the world. Meg Fulton was the most selfless woman he'd ever met. She faced her fears—hell, conquered them—and came to the hospital to see him. She had to still love him, or at least care for him. Damn. What a fool. For months, he'd talked up his former best friend, anxious for his approval of the woman he loved the woman he…*shit*, the woman he wanted to marry.

Now all he had to do was convince Meg that Spiller would never enter her life again, and pray she didn't still see her rapist's face every time she looked at him.

Unable to focus, Meg took the next week off of school. There was still a lot of work to do in the summer, but she had the luxury of picking and choosing which days she wanted off. She and Emma spent time at the Tucker farm, caring for and riding the horses. After a month of self-pity, it felt wonderful to be outdoors with her daughter. It being difficult to carry on a conversation while riding, or rather racing, through fields and trails made it an even more pleasant experience. She admired Emma's spunk and brutal honesty.

Her daughter didn't let her mope around. One day of crying, one day of venting, and then her pride-and-joy demanded she take her life back. Meg couldn't tell Emma or Annie the real reason for the breakup. She stuck with her cover story of caring for Connor, but he'd not been the right one. If that was the case, she needed to act the part. So there she was, horseback riding through lush, green woods. The horses slowed near Pearl Stream to take a drink and then Misty, Meg's older mare, followed Emma's horse, Lady, through the river.

"Emma, don't you think we should head back now?"

"Let's follow the stream out to the lake. I heard it's beautiful out there." Emma called over her left shoulder.

"Honey, I'm sure it is, but we haven't a clue where we are; we've been out here for an hour. I'm not going to be able to walk tomorrow. Much less drive home tonight."

"Lady knows the way." She patted her horse and kicked her heels into its belly.

Meg had never ridden down to the lake before. And she had no desire to today. She needed to work on her plan to get Connor back. Betsy notified her when he got home from the hospital two days ago, but she hadn't mustered up the courage to talk with him yet. He needed time to heal his wounds, physical and emotional, before she told him about J.T. Spiller. Maybe tomorrow.

The stream opened up to the lake. The north end of the lake had a noise ordinance, but the sounds of jet skis and motorboats could be heard in the distance. Emma's horse trotted ahead and came to a stop by a small fishing cabin. She turned Lady around and waited for Misty to catch up.

"Hop down, Mom. Rest your legs for a bit."

Meg, grateful for the opportunity to stretch, slid down the horse until she felt steady ground under foot. She stretched her arms and neck and stood at the edge of the water.

"Oh, honey, it's so relaxing here, isn't it?" She heard the shuffle of horse hooves in the sand and turned to discover Emma and the two horses trotting away from her.

"Emma! Where are you going?" The horses didn't slow but disappeared into the brush. "Emma! You get back here right now!" Her screaming seemed futile. Her daughter abandoned her. Meg picked up a small rock and tossed it into the lake. "Now what do I do?" she muttered.

"You could come inside with me."

Startled, Meg turned. *Connor.* Goosebumps worked their way up from her toes to her fingers. Her heart leaped out of her chest, not from fright but from an overload of love she had kept buried inside for the past month, begging to be released. To Connor. Regaining her composure, she smiled at him.

"I have a feeling I've been set up."

He stayed on the front step of the cabin, hands tucked away in his cargo shorts' pockets, looking as handsome as she'd ever seen him, scrapes, bruises, and all. "You're a smart lady."

Meg bit her bottom lip and stared out onto the lake. "It's beautiful out here."

"Mm. Scenery's a bit nicer from over here."

She turned back around and slowly walked toward

him. “How are you feeling?”

“Amazing.”

“Oh.” There were no clouds in the sky, but it dulled in comparison to the brightness of his eyes. God, she missed him. But before they could stand a chance at reuniting, she needed to tell him the truth. “We need to talk.”

“I have a few other things I’d like to do instead.” He came closer until their bodies brushed, lifted her chin, and touched his lips lightly to hers. The goosebumps came back and her heart relaxed, spilling its contents throughout her body. Meg lifted her arms around his neck and drew his head in for a deeper kiss. Calling it magical and toe curling wouldn’t do it justice. Her body tingled and warmed, her mind swimming but perfectly clear.

He came up for air and rested his forehead against hers. “Damn, I missed you.”

Meg dropped her arms, but he held on to her hands, keeping her close. “We do need to talk.”

Connor led her through the screen door and into a quaint room. The floors were old and scuffed, a raggedy braided rug made the small living area cozy. Mounted fish decorated the walls, as did shelves of football trophies and pictures of Connor and his brothers and sister. She would have rather distanced herself by sitting at the chipped Formica kitchen table, but he sat down on a blue plaid couch that had seen better days.

She shimmied by the rustic, log coffee table and sat. Their knees bumped as she settled next to him. Connor was honest, caring, and kind. He wouldn’t be friends with J.T. if he knew about his sordid past. At least, she hoped he wouldn’t. But there was still her lingering doubt of actual events from that night. She said, “No” over and over again, hadn’t she? Could it be possible she was so drunk that she came on to *him?* No. She would never have come on to the high school quarterback. Sex was never an image she had conjured up before that night. Sure she imagined kissing a boy, dreamed about what it would feel like, but she was too young and naive to think about sex.

Waking up in the backseat of his car, alone, cold and sore, she knew what she'd lost. What he'd stolen. Now it was time for her to get it back. Her life.

"I need to tell you something about—"

"I know about J.T.," he said at the same time.

Her spine stiffened as she met his intense gaze. "What do you mean you *know*?"

Connor shifted closer and stroked her cheek with his thumb. "Sweetheart, I know about J.T."

Blinking back tears and gasping for air, her first reaction—besides obvious shock—was anger. "You knew? You *knew* all this time and you never…" she stood up abruptly banging her knee into the coffee table. Rejection was one thing, but for him to have known all along what James—J.T.—had done to her, well, her heart ached from being ripped out of her chest. A stupid, lovesick idiot who was duped not once, but twice. Searching for an escape route through the veil of tears, she stumbled past the battered couch and into the kitchen, sick and confused.

"Hey, hey, hey." Connor jumped to his feet despite his recent injuries and grabbed her arm.

"Let go of me!" Meg twirled around and released her venom. "You bastard! You used me! You knew—"

"Just listen to—"

"Get the hell out of my way! I never want to—" her mouth clamped shut as his lips came down hard over hers. She remained rigid in his arms, fighting the urge to relax and melt into his strength like she wanted to, but he didn't relent. His powerful body enveloped her as he pressed his lips against hers. When she didn't open up to him, he moved his beautiful mouth to her cheek, her neck, her shoulder. Fidgeting, she managed to step back and break the moment. They both panted for air. He grinned. She seethed.

"It's the only way to shut you up. You have two choices. Listen to what I have to say, or I'll have to go back to restraint. Or I'll tickle you until you snort." He wiggled his eyebrows and looked down at her lips.

Stuck in the middle of nowhere with no transportation, she sighed and plopped herself down on the hard, uncomfortable 1970s kitchen chair. "Go on."

"With the kissing or the talking?" he teased, but she didn't smile. Men like Connor and James were used to getting away with…rape…because of their looks. No. Connor could never be compared to him. No matter how hard she tried, they had nothing in common. Remembering their first big fight over miscommunication, she crossed her arms and listened.

"I found out a few days ago. I finally put all the pieces of your complex puzzle together. I flew down to Texas, dealt with him and then flew back here to see you. Only I got sidetracked on my way home and had to stay in the hospital for a few days." He inched his chair closer and reached out for both of her hands. "He'll never hurt you again, Meg. I swear."

"I—" she peered out from under her lashes and saw the love in his eyes. She sniffed, "What do you mean you *dealt* with him?"

He examined their joined hands and held up his right hand. "It took a car to beat me up. It only took my fist to make him look like this."

"He's your friend—"

"No. He's not. I made it clear he's never welcome near me, you, or Emma, much less the state of New Hampshire, again."

"Emma? You told him about Emma! Oh my God, Connor. He'll try to contact her." Meg ripped her hands out of his grasp. "He's rich. He'll hire the best lawyers and…and sue me. I hid Emma from him. He'll use that, Connor."

"Hey, hey, hey." He soothed again pulling her into his embrace. This time she didn't resist, resting her head on his shoulder and soaking his shirt with her tears. "I took care of it. Trust me."

She picked up her head but stayed in his cocoon. "How?" She wiped her eyes on his shoulder. "How can you promise me he won't try to hurt Emma?"

Connor kissed her forehead and each swollen eye. His tenderness weakened her knees and warmed her heart. "My lawyer sent him some papers and he signed them." He kissed her chin and dipped his head to her most sensitive spot behind her ear. Tingles shot through her body, and she couldn't help but shiver.

"Stop." She attempted to sound serious. "You can't do this to me right now, Connor."

"Okay, later then?"

"Not until you explain it all to me. Now stop distracting or delaying or whatever you're doing and lay the cards on the table."

He released her and walked over to the fridge pulling out a bottle of wine. "Care for a glass?" Not waiting for a response, he took down two completely out of place crystal wineglasses and poured the chilled chardonnay. "Strawberries?" Seemingly out of nowhere, he brought out a tray of enormous chocolate covered strawberries.

Completely baffled, Meg rubbed her hands across her face. "Connor McKay! Stop eluding and tell me what's going on!" The seductive combination of wine, chocolate, and Connor rattled and distracted her from the pressing matter at hand.

Dangling a ripe strawberry in front of her mouth, Connor whispered, "Take a bite." She sighed but complied. He purposely waited for her mouth to be full of rich, dark chocolate and sweet strawberry before adding,

"I'm adopting Emma."

Choking on the delectable duo, Meg braced a hand on her chest and coughed. She swiped up the wineglass and downed nearly half of it before coming up for air and noticing the twinkle in Connor's eyes. "What?" she barked.

"Here." He shoved, not politely, the rest of the strawberry in her mouth. She could choose to either open up or end up with chocolate all over her face. Death by chocolate was not on the agenda for tonight. "J.T. signed the papers and faxed them to my lawyer last night. Emma signed them this morning so all that's left is your John Hancock. Wine?" He held up her glass as if expecting her to choke again.

She didn't choke but took the offered glass and emptied it. Reclaiming her demeanor, she set down the glass, braced her hands on her hips, and rolled her eyes at the ignorant man standing before her.

"So, you adopt my twenty-two-year-old daughter and figure you've solved all my problems? You don't need to be the knight-in-shining-armor, Connor. I truly appreciate you for wanting to help, but I'll find a way. I always do."

"Yes, Meg, you do. You always come out on top, one of my favorite places for you to be." He smirked. She lightly punched his ribs. "Ouch! I'm broken, remember?"

"Yes, I remember. And although I'd love to fix you, I can't. And you can't *fix* my problems by adopting Emma. She's an adult and doesn't need to be adopted. I just need James Spiller to stay away from her."

"He will. The papers are cut and dried. He can't step foot in New Hampshire without letting us know first. He won't come anywhere near our family."

Their eyes met, his tender, hers sad. "Connor, this is all wrong. You can't adopt her. It would be weird. It's not like we're—"

"Married?" Her cheeks flushed. "Let's make it right,

Meg. Marry me."

"Connor." She rested her hands on his chest and picked at an imaginary loose thread. "You're a wonderful man. I care about you a great deal, but I can't let you throw your life away because you feel guilty about telling James about Emma."

"Whoa there, babe. My wanting to marry you has *nothing* to do with him. *Nothing.* And it has nothing to do with gallantry. I want you. Bad. The moment you stepped into my high school all high and mighty, I knew you would give me a run for my money. You put up with all of my idiosyncrasies; you call me out on all the crap I say and do, making an honest man out of me. You're smart, beautiful, kind, loving, and I can't sleep at night without you next to me. And hell, waking up without you is a bitch." He gathered up her loose mane of hair and pulled it away from her face. "I hate mornings when you're not there. So, no, Meg, this proposal has nothing to do with gallantry, but one hundred percent selfishness. I need you. I want you. I love you. And that's all there is to it." He let out a huff of air and looked at her matter-of-factly.

The room went silent, the air thick with emotions, and Meg laughed. "You, Connor McKay, try so hard to be the tough guy, but you're a romantic at heart." She beamed up at him, cradled his face in her hands, and then kissed him slowly and sensuously. The magnetic force pulled their bodies into one solid mass. He kissed her, swallowing her up with his mouth and walked backward, to where, she didn't have a clue, but she'd follow him anywhere.

They ended up in a small, dark bedroom and quickly fell onto an uncomfortable mattress, springs bore into her back, but she didn't feel a thing.

"So is that a yes?" he asked, his mouth still on hers.

"That's a yes," she said as she slid his T-shirt over his head.

Epilogue

"I'm ready when you are." Connor put his left hand into a baseball glove and tapped it with his right fist. "Come on babe, fire away." He squatted at the foot of her hospital bed in a catcher's stance.

"Connor McKay. You get away from there right now! You're not funny!" Meg used her elbows to prop herself up in an attempt to stare over her rounded belly.

He could barely see the top of her head, the pitcher's mound that had once been a flat belly held his precious cargo, and he was more antsy than anxious, more excited than nervous. Being a father didn't scare him in the least.

"I'm getting ready for the big game," he teased.

"Yeah, well they better have heads like little baseballs because if they come out with a head as swollen as yours and shoulders as wide, I'm going to kill you. Now wipe that goofy grin off your face and grab me a cold cloth. I'm dying here."

The nurse who was prepping for the arrival of his babies chuckled and walked out the door.

More than happy to dote on his extremely pregnant and incredibly moody wife, Connor rinsed the white washcloth in the stainless steel sink and wrung out the excess water. He tri-folded it just the way Meg asked—or, demanded—last time and gently placed it on her forehead, followed by a soft kiss to her nose.

"You're beautiful."

"I'm fat."

"You're pregnant."

"Seriously, Connor. Twins? Can you ever do anything half-ass?"

"Tsk, tsk. Such vulgar words from the mother of my children. And no, only the best for my wife. You're doing great. Dr. Sherman thinks you'll be ready to push within the hour."

"Hand!"

He knew the drill. Connor sacrificed his right hand—his left still wore the catcher's mitt—and felt his bones crunch under Meg's intense squeeze.

"Ahh!" she screamed. "I need to push. NOW!"

He soothed comforting words in her ear and reached up to stroke her hair, but the damn mitt got in the way. So much for trying to lighten the mood. After a minute of intense bone crunching, he ran out into the hall and called for the doctor. He hated to hear his wife in so much pain and knowing he couldn't do a damned thing to help made him feel worse. The comedy routine helped take her mind off the contractions for a while, but in the past hour they had gotten stronger and faster. Meg's eyes were bloodshot; she shivered and sweated at the same time, and seemed to have lost all sense of hearing. He stood by her side and whispered encouraging words as she grunted, screamed, trembled, and panted.

Ninety minutes of sailor swearing, Freddy Krueger screaming, and ten broken fingers all ended with the final push of their little girl. Meg cradled her twins, Tucker Randall and Hannah Grace, to her chest and smiled.

Connor had never been so blessed, so happy, so in love. "They're beautiful and perfect," he whispered in his wife's ear. "Just like you."

Can't get enough of the
McKay-Tucker Men?
Turn the page to enjoy an excerpt from

False Hope

McKay-Tucker Men Book 2

Chapter One

"Higher. Oh, God, right there. Yes! Oh, harder. Faster!" Emma Fulton closed her eyes and trembled beneath his warm, calloused hands. His long, strong legs straddled her, pinning her into the couch. She felt him easing from her and yelled, "Don't you dare stop, Cole Tucker! You've got the spot…right…there…oh…my…" She arched under him, moaned, and let out a long sigh before going limp. "Oh, that felt so damned good."

"Was it as good for you as it was for me?"

"Better."

The weight of his body quickly left her, and she heard him growl, "Damn. My balls are cold."

Rolling over onto her back, Emma sat up on the couch and scowled. "You're such a pig."

"What?" Cole grinned and winked. "My meatball sub was nice and toasty warm before you asked me to scratch your itch." He winked at his innuendo.

"Well, so-rry." Emma smacked his shoulder. "I can't reach that far." She stretched her arm over her head trying to get to the magic spot beneath her shoulder blade where the damn mosquito bit her last night and drained her of nearly a quart of blood.

"Poptart, you keep making noises like that and the neighbors are gonna start pounding down your door."

"You are my neighbor, wiseass."

"Yeah." Cole kissed her forehead. "Lucky me."

Emma tied her long, brown hair up with an elastic band and glanced up at the clock.

"I told my mom we'd be at her place at two. It's quarter past, and you're eating a sub. I'll never understand men." She snorted in disgust and walked into her kitchen, opening the fridge and taking out the bowl of pasta salad she made for the family barbecue.

Cole licked sauce from his fingers and wiped them on his khaki shorts, earning a scowl from Emma.

"It's an appetizer. We menfolk need lots of protein to help us keep up with our…extra-curricular activities." He tugged on her ponytail and grabbed the bowl of pasta salad from her.

"You're a cocky little boy. Now let's go," she teased, tossing a checkered pillow at him.

"Boy? Want me to show you how much of a man I am?"

"No thanks!" She laughed and grabbed her purse. "You're driving. It's my turn to get liquored up."

Cole followed her out the door and to his truck. "Does this mean I get to take advantage of you tonight?"

She snorted. "I'm not planning on getting *that* drunk."

The small country roads of Newhall, New Hampshire, were nearly desolate. It wasn't a town that attracted summer tourists, leaf peepers, or winter skiers. Most bypassed the uneven, pothole-ridden roads on their drive to the White Mountains, which the townsfolk appreciated. It wouldn't have appealed to Emma as a teenager, but leaving Boston at twenty-two and moving to the small town six years ago with her mother had been the best thing for her family. Not that she had much of a family before her mother married Cole's older half-brother, Connor McKay.

Connor loved Meg more than life itself, and soon after he married Emma's mom, they became pregnant with twins. Emma loved her little brother and sister more than life itself. Between them, Connor, and his extended family, Emma and Meg had never been happier. Since blending their families, Cole had become one of her best friends. He and Emma were the most alike. They lived adjacently to each other in one of the duplexes the Tuckers owned and had the same interests. Sports, socializing, the outdoors, and a good night out. Mason, though, was another story. He may have been Cole's identical twin, but outside of physical appearance, all similarities ended there.

Mason was aloof, serious, and anything but social. In the handful of years Emma had been part of the McKay-Tucker clan, she had yet to figure him out.

Cole pulled up to her mother and Connor's waterfront home where her two most favorite people in the world greeted them. Hannah's blonde pigtails swung back and forth as her little legs pumped hard to beat her twin brother, Tucker, to the truck.

"Sissy!" Her smile grew as she leaped into Emma's arms.

"Hey, princess. I missed you! Why, I think you've grown since I saw you last week!" Emma kissed Hannah's nose, shifted the little body in her arms, and then whispered in her ear. "Are you wearing big girl undies?"

"Yeah, just like you. Wanna see?" Hannah squirmed out of Emma's arms and lifted her pink sundress, revealing Cinderella underwear. "They're princess undies. Do you have princess undies?"

"Yeah, Sissy, show us your undies," Cole teased behind her.

Ignoring him, Emma whispered in Hannah's ear.

"I'm very proud of you, princess. You let me know if you have to go pee on the potty. Okay?"

Cole scooped up Hannah and put her on his shoulders.

"She peed on the floor this morning and Daddy stepped in it," Tucker said. "It was disgusting." He was only four, but he tried really hard to act like one of "the boys." Granted "the boys" worked pretty hard at acting like they were four.

Cole looked up at his little niece perched high on his shoulders. "Don't pee on Uncle Cole, okay, princess?"

Emma hid her smile and kneeled in front of her little brother. "Well, Mister Man, I recall not long ago when a certain young, dark-haired, blue-eyed, little-big brother had a few accidents of his own." Tucker loved being the big brother, even if it was by a mere three minutes, and tried to act like he didn't like being Emma's *little* brother. "You helping Dad with the grill tonight?"

"Yup. He said we can make s'mores later too."

"Cool." She reached for his hand and walked around the house to the lake in the back where the fun had already started.

"Sissy and Uncole are here!" Hannah shouted from her perch. Her blending of Uncle and Cole would never grow tiresome. Of course the grown-ups twisted Hannah's endearment to *Uncool.*

Cole sauntered up to Meg with one of his typical pickup lines. "Your beauty makes the morning sun look like the dull glimmer of the moon." He hugged Emma's mom and kissed her cheek.

Emma rolled her eyes. Meg, Emma's mother—although many would say she resembled an older sister—smiled.

"Hi, kids." She took the bowl from Emma and gave her a warm, one-armed hug. "We've got chowder, every salad under the sun, and lots of sweets. The boys only eat meat, chips, and beer at these gatherings, so the rest is up to us. Hope you're hungry."

"Starved. What can I do to help? Is Paige here yet?" Paige and Emma had become instant best friends when Emma and her mom first moved to Newhall. Ironically, the first friend Meg had made was Annie, Paige's mom and Connor's sister. Rick, Annie's husband, was a quiet psychiatrist who never psychoanalyzed but was always there when someone needed a confidant.

"She, Annie, and Rick are riding over in the boat. Connor went fishing with Mason and their dad, but they should be back soon. Feel like going for a swim? The kids have been asking to go."

"Sure. I just need to go in and change."

The women walked into the house while Cole popped open a beer and played with his little nephew and niece. The house was always welcoming, a little different from back in the day when Connor lived in it as a bachelor. Landmines of Legos, Barbies, and trucks littered corners of the house. Artwork covered the stainless steel fridge and feminine touches like candles, curtains, and primitive framed prints softened the massive house and made it feel like a loving home.

Emma envied her mother, not the first thirty-six years of her mother's life, but every moment after. Since Meg met Connor, her life changed into a fairytale. An amazing father, a popular teacher, a kickass coach, and the most devoted, loyal husband any woman could dream of. Finding true love had never been on Emma's to-do list. She didn't think it would even make her bucket list either.

She'd had her share of relationships, never without a date or a list of eligible candidates, but no one ever made her think about happily ever after. And at twenty-eight, she was too young to be thinking about forever. It was her time to play the field, sow her wild oats, something her mother never got the chance to do. In another five or six years, she'd start thinking about the white dress and the trip down the aisle. Maybe. For now it was all fun and games, exactly how she liked it.

"I have some bathing suits Tracy sent me I wouldn't be caught dead wearing." Meg laughed at Emma's scowl and redirected. "Because I don't have the body I once had before those twins stretched me like a hot air balloon. I'm too old to be flitting around in bikinis." Meg dug out a bag from the back of her closet and pulled out a few bathing suits, tags still attached.

"I'm sure Connor would disagree," Emma teased. "Oh, these are cute. I'll take the green halter top one." She went into the master bath to change.

Tracy had been her mother's best friend since they met in college. Tracy, being gay, and Meg, a very young sixteen-year-old college freshman with a baby, made them the perfect odd couple. He had majored in fashion design and obtained a job as a stylist in New York City while Meg had majored in science education and parenting 101. The two had been best friends ever since. Uncle Tracy somehow managed to fit in and befriend the McKay-Tucker testosterone-filled family.

The side benefit of the relationship was a closet chocked full of designer duds both Meg and Emma barely wore. When Emma was in high school, she'd loved the new clothes Tracy sent. But they didn't serve much purpose in college or in her current job as a physical therapist. Her mother wore the business suits but didn't have much need for the cocktail dresses and evening gowns. And Emma's fashion sense leaned more toward athletic shorts and a pair of Nikes.

"So, Em, are you and Cole getting along okay? I mean, living next door to each other?"

"Yeah, it's been a lot of fun. Granted I've only been living there for two months." Emma emerged from the bathroom in the new Dolce & Gabbana suit. Her mother dressed in a slimming, black one-piece and wraparound skirt.

"And are you two…"

"Friends, Mom. He's like a brother to me." No one could deny how incredibly hot and suave Cole Tucker was. His magnetic charm was what made them best friends. But they'd never had any serious sexual chemistry.

"I know, but you dated before, and I thought…well, since you're practically in the same house…"

"Mom, we almost hooked up for like two seconds. We never dated." She put air quotes around the word. "And we're not roommates. It's a duplex. We're cool."

"Uh, huh," she said skeptically.

"Whatever, come on, let's take the kids for a swim."

They changed Hannah and Tucker into their swimsuits and waded out into the lake. The cool water felt refreshing with the July sun beating down on her shoulders. Hannah clung to Emma's legs, not wanting to risk falling down in the water while Tucker tested out his water wings. There was so much splashing and laughing they hardly heard the canoe dock beside them.

"There are my favorite grandkids," George Tucker called, barely waiting for Connor and Mason to tie up the boat before climbing out.

"Bumpa!" they yelled and splashed.

Hannah attached herself like a barnacle to Emma. "Carry me to Grampy, Emma!"

"Hey, Bumpa, catch anything?" Emma asked.

"A couple of grandkids." He chuckled as Tucker climbed up his grandfather's body. "Found another kid and grandkid out on the lake." He winked. Paige and her parents pulled up in their fishing boat and docked behind him.

"Hey, you." Paige hopped out of the boat and jumped into the water to hug Emma. "I haven't seen you lately."

"Sorry. Busy with the new job, moving in, and all. How's summer vacation so far?"

"Awesome." Paige kissed Hannah on the head. "I get to see my cousins and hopefully my best friend. One of the perks of teaching—summers off."

"Yeah, well, I still can't believe you came back here to teach with your mom and Connor and all your old teachers. It's just too weird. But I'm thrilled to have you back home." Emma set Hannah down in the water. After graduating from the University of New Hampshire, Paige had wanted to explore a little and took a job teaching abroad in Japan. But she missed her friends and family and returned to Newhall a few weeks ago, landing a teaching job in her former elementary school.

"It's been sort of weird this past week, setting up my classroom and talking with Mrs. Bertrand. Who, by the way, has to be at least eighty. She was old when I had her in second grade. Besides, it's not like I'm at the high school. First grade is a far cry from the good ol' days at NHS. So…" Paige looked over her shoulder at Mason and then up on the lawn at Cole. "How do you liking living with Cole? You guys hook up yet?"

Emma rolled her eyes. "Geesh, will everyone get over it already? We're not living together, and we're just friends."

"Friends that—"

"Don't you dare say it Paige Thorne," she growled.

"Okay, okay, calm down." Paige laughed. "I can see it's a *touchy* subject."

Emma trudged out of the water to their towels. She dried off her sister and wrapped her in a giant princess towel. "Want Sissy to get you dressed, princess, or do you want to stay in your bathing suit?"

"I want to swim with Uncle Mason."

"Oh," Emma said, surprised. He stood on the dock by the boat putting the fishing poles away. She scooped up the princess cocoon and went to him.

"Hi, Mason."

He eyed her abruptly, up, then down, and then back up again. She wasn't sure if he was checking her out or if he was simply nervous. "Hi…Emma. Hey, Hannah Banana." A weak smile appeared on his lips for his niece.

"I wanna swim wif you," Hannah said, reaching out her arms to him.

"Oh, okay." Mason took her awkwardly in his arms and unwrapped the towel dropping it on the dock. He stripped out of his shirt and shoes and carried his niece to the water, ignoring Emma. "Want to walk on my feet again?"

Emma couldn't help it if her eyes bugged out and latched on to his pecks. *Where has he been hiding those?* As he waded in deeper, his trunks soaked up the lake water and molded beautifully to his perfect backside.

Emma wasn't sure what to make of the image. She never really connected with Mason during their family gatherings. But her eyes sure as heck connected now. Shortly after she moved to Newhall, he had left to go to grad school and then lived in New York City. He came home for holiday events, but never struck up conversations with Emma. Instead, he avoided her.

Where Cole was an extrovert in every way possible, Mason was the exact opposite—an introvert to the extreme. Or at least toward her. A computer genius with a prestigious job as a computer hacker, a legal one, companies from all over New England called for Mason's services, or so she heard. Computers were not her forte. That six-pack and sexy v-thing had to mean serious gym time or a crazy-ass sports addiction. The burst of desire in her belly confused and delighted her.

Mason and Cole were identical twins. They had the same short, black hair, dark chocolate eyes, and Matt Damon dimples. Cole's physique mirrored his brother's, so why did the quiet one turn her head?

Rolling her tongue back in her mouth, Emma turned and went inside, suddenly feeling very exposed.

After changing back into her jean shorts and pink spaghetti strap tank, she combed out her hair and pulled it back into a ponytail—her go-to hairstyle. While her mother exuded style and confidence, Emma rocked the comfortable style. The irony of it was that Meg Fulton McKay *was* the most insecure woman known to mankind and used her style—compliments of personal shopper and best friend Tracy James—to mask her weaknesses while Emma felt strong and competent and couldn't care less what she looked like. But for some reason, unbeknownst to her—or so she told herself—she pawed through her mother's makeup bag and applied a touch of mascara and a coat of lip gloss. It had nothing to do with the fact that the incredibly delicious Mason happened to be outside swimming with Hannah. No, nothing at all.

Author's Bio:

Marianne Rice grew up flip-flopping between southern California and southern New Hampshire. Nope. Not an army brat. Just a lot of life changes (which is great fodder for her books!) Talk about culture shock! She's a city girl when it comes to style, but a country girl at heart.

She spends her time transporting her three kids to cheering, soccer, field hockey, basketball, lacrosse, and baseball. She works a full-time job, is a part-time chauffeur, a full-time cook/baker/cleaner, and a part-time writer. Math isn't her specialty, but she's working on her ratios and percentages, hoping to change a few things around.

MarianneRice.com

Other books in the McKay-Tucker Series

False Hope
False Impressions

Made in the USA
Middletown, DE
06 January 2023